Smelling Lilac

Ambrose E. Korn Jr.

Copyright © 2018 Ambrose E. Korn Jr.

2nd Edition

All rights reserved, including the right to reproduce this book, or portions thereof in any form. No part of this text may be reproduced, transmitted, downloaded, decompiled, reverse engineered, or stored, in any form or introduced into any information storage and retrieval system, in any form or by any means, whether electronic or mechanical without the express written permission of the author.

This is a work of fiction. Names and characters are the product of the author's imagination and any resemblance to actual persons, living or dead, is entirely coincidental.

The views expressed in this work are solely those of the author and do not necessarily reflect the views of the publisher, and the publisher hereby disclaims any responsibility for them.

ISBN: 978-1-387-64622-7

PublishNation LLC
www.publishnation.net

For Denise Ann

*Swiftly taken from family and friends under
a dark Illinois sky*

Acknowledgements

Special thanks to:

Jake Korn for character Ben's 5th grade poem.

Jamie Wincovich for living in a geeky flawlessness world and like a sign post pointing me there also.

Prologue

Tim peeped from underneath the blanket. The morning light was dim. He could see his inverted sailor's cap sitting on top of his underwear. A little further along was the rest of his white uniform crumpled into a pile on the cane-matted floor. In the hollow of the cap he could see his black wallet and the wrinkled envelope that held his letter from Sarah. He'd received the letter aboard ship weeks ago while still at sea. He'd read it over and over and by now he could recite it by memory. Why he'd carried the painful written words along with him on shore leave he did not know.

He raised his cheek up from the hard mattress and poked his head out from under the blanket. He looked for the prostitute. He was alone in the whorehouse bed. He let his head drop slowly back onto the mattress and pulled the blanket back over his head.

He was beginning to doze off when he heard the sliding door to the room open and then close. The young Chinese girl slithered under the covers and lay motionless beside him. Sometime during the intoxicating night he gave her his innocence. Now the purity he struggled to keep bundled up for Sarah alone was gone from his life, just as Sarah was gone from his life.

Perhaps by bringing her letter to the whorehouse, he felt that Sarah was with him when he quit being an altar boy and blew out the candle of make-believe. Dead and gone were the happily-ever-after dreams of being forever with Sarah. He would leave her letter in this Hong Kong whorehouse along with his long held belief that Sarah could love only him. He turned and caressed the beauty and softness of Asia.

CHAPTER ONE

Frigid morning storms are the worst way winter days can begin. Father Tim Brogan was sure of that as he turned his car onto the snow covered parking lot. He pressed down hard on the brake and the car slid to one side and to a stop. He shifted into park and turned the headlights off. Tim laid his face down against the plastic steering wheel letting the engine idle and stereo play. It felt good closing his eyes after the long drive. Soft music caressed his soul.

Wind shook the little car, snow piled up on the windows, shutting out the world. He had lived through the painful loss of Sarah's love years ago and filled that emptiness in his heart with learning and music. He started to cry. Across the parking lot and inside the funeral home was Sarah's corpse tempting him to view her remains and go mad. He would not find God today, only music.

When the music finished, he lifted his tired head and took a handkerchief from the inside of his coat pocket to wipe his face. He saw himself in the rear view mirror. He looked dirty, maybe he even smelled. He needed a shave; his square jaw was covered with heavy brown stubble. The whites of his eyes were pink and the light blue had no sparkle. His face had the empty look, the shell shocked look of a soldier after a bloody battle. Sarah had understood that face that now looked tired and worn. She had kissed it, caressed it, and laughed at the nonsense that came out of its mouth. She had stared into its eyes with concern whenever his mood became serious, thinking confusing thoughts of life that so often befuddled him, thoughts she could easily send away with a kiss.

He sighed and raised his black coat collar around his neck. After a moment of hesitation, he opened the car door. Blasting cold air hit his hands and face as he crawled from the car into the blowing snow of February. He shook from a chill that ran over his body and with careful steps began his walk to Sarah. Neither the thin socks nor the black dress shoes he wore could keep the cold or wetness from his feet. He reached the front door of the funeral home and leaned against the splintered old wood that framed the door. With a cold hand, he turned the knob. The door creaked and opened to warm air that smelled like flowers. Tim shut the door on the storm.

The passageway to the viewing rooms was wallpapered, a sconce on the wall before each parlor had a dim amber bulb in its socket. Tim let out a heavy sigh. The walk down the hallway was going to be hard. His pants were shaking from knee quivers. He just stood there feeling weak and fell back against the front door while melting snow ran from his head and coat onto the carpeted floor. He wiped his cold hand hard over his face, straightened up, and tried to walk with some sort of dignity to Sarah.

A painful gasp escaped from his throat at the sight of Sarah in her coffin. He walked up close to her corpse. Tim recognized the red rosary laced through her fingers as the one he had sent to her as a gift from Central America years ago. He reached out and touched her hand. It was hard. He jerked his hand away, jolted by the stiffness in the hand that had held his so tenderly in the past and in his dreams every day of his life since they parted. He collapsed onto the kneeler in front of the coffin. Sarah was dead. She could not laugh, or curse, or cry anymore. She had gone to God and all that would be left for Tim were memories. But that was all he'd really ever had since he left her. How stupid he had been for leaving her side and choosing to live forevermore in a wanton state of mind.

He arose from the kneeler, angry with himself. He could never get comfortable kneeling and avoided that unnatural position as much as possible. He walked across the parlor and slumped into a comfortable chair and viewed her from a distance. Baskets of fresh cut flowers were positioned around the coffin. He had not sent any flowers. His eyes were tired and wet and losing focus. He turned his head to the cracked stained glass window; it was a depiction of Michelangelo's hand of God reaching out to Adam. Adam had Eve by his side when he was cast out of Eden. Adam had not been so foolish as to cast himself from paradise. That is what Tim had done to himself, banished himself from paradise when he left Sarah. Anger was boiling up in his stomach. He did not want to look at Sarah again. He did not want to remember her in her coffin. He thought he should have stayed at the seminary.

Tim's body began to sag in the chair. His eyelids were heavy. He rubbed his face hard to stay awake. Suddenly, he thought of John. John was dead also. That's what Bonnie had said when she called him at the seminary. She said that the both of them were dead. In his sorrow over Sarah, his unlimited daydreaming over how it had been between the two of them, he'd completely forgotten about his friend John.

Tim leaned back in the chair and closed his eyes. He wondered what time it was, but was too tired to lift his arms or open his eyes to look at his watch. Sleep began to come to him in bits and pieces, and then settled upon him. Darkness comforted him and his dreams. The sounds of strange music filtered through his brain, Japanese music. Japanese people and Big John, all danced in circles like drunken fools, spreading their arms while singing and laughing.

Streams of vague pictures floated in his mind. Paper sliding doors, satin slit dress, smooth bronze body, long black hair, kissing, crawling, hot green tea, Big John laughing…a hand was on his arm. It was rough and pulling.

"What…?"

"Father, wake up!" The old undertaker was speaking to him. "The funeral home isn't open for visitation."

"Yes, yes, I'm going. Sorry I came before scheduled hours."

Tim felt as stiff as Sarah's hand. His neck was sore from hanging over the back of the chair. "Do you remember me, Mr. Reilly? I'm Father Brogan, you handled the arrangements for my parents, their burials."

"Yeah, yeah," the old man said taking Tim by the arm. "You got to go."

The small undertaker's dark brown suit coat hung on him loosely and looked to the priest to be many times worn and frayed. "What time is it?" Tim asked.

"Almost seven," the undertaker barked and started pulling on Tim's arm. Tim followed, sheepishly, being escorted to the front door. "And get some rest, Father, you look like hell!"

"Wait!" Tim moaned. "Where's John's body? Sarah's husband." Tim stopped and pulled away from Mr. Reilly's weak grip.

"He's on the elevator, waiting to be brought upstairs. Come on, you can't see him now."

"But I must," Tim raised his voice. I drove all the way from New York. I'm a teacher at a seminary there."

Mr. Reilly interrupted him. "Soooo, get some rest and come back this afternoon." Then added sarcastically. "We're open in the evening too…you know!"

Tim had already made up his mind. He wasn't staying for their funerals; he was getting out of town after catching a few hours sleep at Saint James rectory. Why torment himself?

"Sir," Tim spoke softly and lied right into the old man's steely eyes. "I have a class of young missionaries graduating tomorrow morning. Then being sent on their often dangerous assignments around the world to bring the word of God to pagans. After a short rest at Saint James' rectory, I'm heading back to New York. If I don't see John now to say my goodbye, well, I just won't see him. Sir, I'll leave if you insist, but those two people were my friends and very big supporters in my missionary work."

The undertaker studied Tim's face. He hated people interfering with his work, and his was a delicate business, it wasn't right for outsiders to view the body before family.

Tim added to his lie. "And I need to pray over John's body, like I did for Sarah."

"What? I didn't hear no praying, only snoring! Come on, but make it quick. Understand?"

Tim nodded and followed behind the slow walking undertaker down a flight of stairs and through a few doors into the laboratory. John's coffin was closed and on the elevator. Mr. Reilly opened the lid and barked. "Well, let's go, pray."

Tim stared at the old man hard. "Aren't you being a little rude?"

"Me? What about you, barging into my funeral home before I even had a chance to do my job? What do you want from me this early in the morning? Cereal and cheerfulness?"

"No!" Tim snapped. "Five minutes alone. How can I say meaningful prayers with you hovering over the casket and shooing me away, in your rush to slam the coffin lid shut as if it were the trunk of your car?"

"Five minutes, then out you go." The undertaker turned and walked off of the elevator and went away through one of the doors in the room.

Tim did not touch John's hands, but he studied them. Even the undertaker's solvents could not improve the appearance of John's hard working hands. They were a mechanics hands, callused, nicked and cut, split fingernails, and never thoroughly clean. In their youth, John was the tinkering kid of the gang. He enjoyed engines; tearing them apart, rebuilding them, and making them hum to a recognizable pitch until the sound was perfect to his ear. If John had a philosophy about life, Tim was never told it. If he harbored any jealousy over Sarah's past involvement with him, it was never revealed to the priest.

John looked asleep, not dead. He looked uncomfortable being so big and stuffed into a box obviously not made to order. John's arms were long and his big hands were crossed over his crotch. Tim thought his hands should be moved to his sides. He too held a rosary, but Tim knew it wasn't John's. It was probably furnished by the funeral home, an automatic. Catholic, one stock rosary, please. Protestant, one crucifix. Idol hating evangelist, one plain wooden cross. But, John wasn't Catholic, or any sort of a Christian. John never searched about for God, while Tim was always trying to sneak a peep through the clouds.

Tim often wondered why John was so different from himself and the others that they grew up around. He was never rude, quick to smile, strong as an ox and docile as a lamb. He was always forgiving, the exception being his mother. But otherwise kind and a model Christian in every way except belief. They had gone to Catholic grade school together, but he'd told Tim later in life that he did not believe in God. He never changed his mind as far as the priest knew. What Brogan did know was that his dead pal had been a good and honest man and he prayed that God in his judgment would be merciful.

John's black hair was beginning to gray and Tim was studying its healthy fullness compared to his own thinning crop at forty-three when Mr. Reilly appeared in a huff. "Time's up!"

"Gosh," Tim chuckled. "Where's your stopwatch?"

"Cute. Let's go!"

Tim was walked to the front door. "By the way, Mr. Reilly," Tim whispered, "do you think you could move John's hands away from his fly?"

The front door shut behind Tim. Freezing wind hit his face. He looked up at the sky. It had stopped snowing. Brogan took in the view of his hilly hometown. Wind howled through the naked branches of the trees lining the road. The street was clogged with morning traffic, bumper to bumper, lined up like an amusement park ride inching along to the fast track.

He had no urgent work at the seminary, but still wanted to return soon. There was nothing for him in Rivers Bend anymore, only painful memories. He just stood there freezing in front of Mr. Reilly's funeral home thinking about the other snowy days, and the other winds that howled when he and Sarah had played in the snow. He mumbled to her. "It was a new snow then to Sarah. We wrote messages in it. We wrote our dreams in it." Tears ran down his face. He didn't wipe them away, only put his hands in his pockets and walked away from Sarah. Over his shoulder he whispered his love for her in Spanish, "Mi amor para ti es eterno, Sarah." Tim tried to chuckle but choked on it. She loved it when he talked to her in Spanish.

CHAPTER TWO

Seaman Brogan could smell the repugnant odor of the fish market he just passed. It stayed in his nostrils even when he entered the smoke and whiskey smelling bar. He could not understand the chubby little woman behind the bar, but it was plain to him that she was lecturing the young girls perched on a row of stools in front of the long bar. The chubby Japanese woman looked up at Tim standing there with his sailor cap in hand.

"Goo affanoon."

Tim smiled. "I'm looking for a girl, Kimiko?"

A tall slender girl stood up and came to him. She was smiling and beautiful. "My name Kimiko." Her accent was mild.

He was smitten before she reached his side. The slit up her black satin dress to her hip bone exposed most of her bronze leg as she moved. "Ah, Tim, my..." Before he could finish speaking, Kimiko gave out a shrieking cry.

"Hai! John-san friend." Her lovely face broke into a mouth-opening grin. She covered her mouth with her hand in the custom of the Japanese.

"John, yes John." Tim spoke slowly. "He, John said if I come Iwakuni, come here, this bar, Harrigan's. Ask for Kimiko."

She gave off a sharp, "Hai!" Then turned and spoke in rapid Japanese to the other girls all turned on their stools facing them. They were all dressed similar to Kimiko, slit satin colorful dresses with a lot of leg showing. To Tim, it seemed that they were all talking and giggling at once. While the other girls were still chatting, Kimiko moved closer to Tim, took his sailor cap out of his hands and put in on her head. Her girlfriends all laughed. "Happy met you, Tim-san."

Tim smiled. "Happy met you."

She grabbed Tim by the hand, yelled something to the others and pulled him towards the door. "I take you John-san."

Outside Kimiko hailed a battered taxicab. The back seat was small and Tim had trouble with his long legs. He could feel Kimiko pressed against him. She smiled and leaned forward to speak to the driver.

The driver hit the gas and sped straight ahead. The two were tossed closer together by the cab's jerky acceleration. Kimiko looked like a China doll. Something precisely manufactured. Her long thick black hair was cut remarkably even midway down her back. She had no blemish on her bronze colored skin. A polished look radiated from her face. Her hands were perfectly formed, manicured and rested on her lap.

She was looking into his light blue eyes. Her own black eyes sparkled as she lifted her fingers to his face. "Eyes, look like sky."

Tim spoke slowly. Chopped up English, a kind of pidgin was getting easier. His ship had docked at enough Far East ports for him to learn that short, terse, twisted English was the best way to communicate with the people he encountered. "John, my friend, long time."

Kimiko nodded. "Hai, Japanese speak tomodachi."

"Tomodachi," Tim repeated.

"Hai." She pointed to her small breast. His eyes followed her hand. "Me, John-san, have uchi. Home. We go now. Not far."

Tim nodded that he understood.

"First come Japan?" Kimiko asked.

"Yes. My ship no come before."

"All seventh fleet ships come Japan before." She was grinning. Her coal colored eyes flashing. He laughed. Kimiko understood every word he spoke, and she gave off a look that said, "I'm smarter than you think American sailor boy.

"You're right, but before I crew member."

They slammed together as the taxi turned a bend. Tim could feel her body heat. They sped across a small stone bridge onto a dirt road and left the village behind. He looked out the window. The countryside was hilly, similar to the terrain of his roots in Western Pennsylvania. Cultivated fields in a tier pattern stepped up and around the hillsides. Off in the distance he could see a pagoda peeking through some late morning mist. He turned back to Kimiko. "Your home Iwakuni?"

"No, Osaka. I come Iwakuni work. Takusan Marine. Takusan Sailor. Takusan yen. Must live. Must work. I help Mama-san. She stay Osaka. I help brother. He stay Tokyo."

"Takusan?" Tim asked.

"Many!" Kimiko spread her hands apart.

He smiled. "Have more takusan Sailors Yokohama, right?"

"Have more takusan bar girls too," Kimiko snapped. "Iwakuni, not so many girls, country place, more yen for me."

Tim nodded. "Your Father?"

"Dead. War."

"I'm sorry."

Kimiko took his hand. "No sorry. He die before war America. Chinese kill. I two years old he die. I don't know him."

Tim had not thought of holding her hand, but now that he was, he didn't want to let go.

Kimiko was still talking. "Nothing can do. Everyone must die."
Tim smiled down on her.

The dirt road was getting to be less like a road and more like a path between rice paddies. Some of the paddies were being worked by bent over people wearing rubber hip boots and pointed straw hats. Their legs were engulfed in both water and plants up to their knees.

"You meet John...Harrigan's bar?"

"Hai. We have good time. Takusan party. John-san party boy."

The taxi stopped. Kimiko shifted exposing most of her leg. They crawled from the cab. After speaking with the driver, Kimiko took Tim by the arm and guided him over a dirt path toward a wooden house. She gave him back his cap.

Two small children, shirtless and barefoot, were running around in front of the house. Kimiko called out to them. They turned and ran to the house and rapped at the door.

"John-san! John-san!" They sang and danced up and down in unison.

Before Kimiko and Tim reached the house, its front slid open and Brogan could see his big buddy in the doorway, barefoot and wearing a bright red kimono embroiled with several mean looking dragons.

"Tim!" John screamed. He slipped his feet into rubber thongs and leaped outside onto the dirt path.

Tim had a rush of a sort that filled him with emotion. It was exhilarating meeting his hometown pal in a foreign country, surrounded by a mysterious culture. In seconds they were hugging each other. Kimiko laughed watching the two men smack each other on the back.

Kimiko said something in Japanese, and John broke away from his Pal and rushed to her side. They spoke for a few moments, and then Kimiko turned from John, returned to the waiting taxi and was driven away.

John grabbed one of the little boys and lifted him to his face. "Tell Mama-san mizu!" He put the boy back on his feet in the dirt. "Hayaku! Hayaku!" He shouted after them as they scrambled over each other to do as John asked, and disappeared to the backside of the house.

"John, buddy, you've gone native."

"Just about, only problem is finding one of these dresses to fit right. Come on in! I'll show you my pad."

John flipped off his thongs and Tim removed his shoes and followed behind John onto the cane matted floor. John put a half-gallon of Canadian whiskey on a low, highly varnished table, and threw a small pillow at Tim. They sat down on the floor next to the table and whiskey.

There was a rap at the sliding door. John heaved his weight onto his hands and knees and crawled to the door and slid it open. Using both hands, the smiling boy handed John a pitcher of water.

"Domo!" John yelled. The lad giggled and ran away. John shut the door. "Well, Tim, whata you think?" John said walking on his knees back to his place at the table.

Tim chuckled seeing his friend walking on his knees, clutching the pitcher of water in his strong hands. "You have gone native!"

"I love it here. I've never been so damn happy. I live like a king." He mixed them both a drink, and then scampered around the room on his knees. He got ice from a small refrigerator and a large ashtray from behind another sliding door.

Tim took a sip. It was strong. "John, do you get homesick?"

"Naw." John gulped half of his drink down his throat.

Tim had a hard time sitting cross-legged like John, and moved his legs around the floor trying to find a less painful position. John ignored his discomfort. "Whata ya think of Kimiko?"

"Beautiful, gracious, stunning, what else can I say? I'm impressed."

"Aah, don't be." John laughed, and waved his big hand in the air as if shooing away Tim's compliment. "Ya know she's a whore, don't you? Takes all my yen, but whata girl, I love the hell outta her."

Tim wasn't surprised by John's statement. Harrigan's was a serviceman's hangout and he'd seen many of them since joining the Navy. Tim lifted his glass, "To home!"

John lifted his glass high. "To the old gang!" and guzzled his drink. Tim did the same. John was pouring them another drink. "Now don't get me wrong about Kimiko, she's no street walker. No sailor with a thousand yen gets that girl's favors. Hell, she pulls in plenty hustling drinks at Harrigan's. She drinks colored water. Those horny sailors and marines off the ships buy her as many drinks as she wants. And she wants a lot. Gets a cut on each drink."

Tim chuckled. "How's her bladder holding up?"

"Christ, Tim, you should see her. She floats around the bar, hustling two or three guys at once, talking, flirting, drinking, and promising herself to them all after the bar closes."

Tim sat his glass down on the table and grinned. "A war child. Must live, must work."

John remained sitting cross-legged like a totem pole while Tim kept shifting his body about the floor hoping to find a comfortable position. "She comes here every night?" Tim asked.

"Sure, we sleep together, lovers of a sort. Only now and then does she go off with a customer after work, if the price is right, and by right,

I mean takusan yen. She always gets word to me if she's not coming home so I don't worry."

Tim lit a cigarette. "While I'm bouncing on the ocean blue, you're here cuddling Kimiko. I should've joined the Marines. Don't any of those guys she hustles ever get angry? Some drunk could hurt her."

"Naw, she slips away before the bar closes, if they're still in port the next day, by then they're sober, and probably got mellowed out by a street walker before goin' back aboard ship."

Tim refilled their glasses and took a deep drag on his cigarette. She makes that good of living drinking colored water?"

John shook his head. "Kimiko convinced me men are assholes."

Tim laughed. "Tell me something new. If you're young and have a penis, you're a moron. The three go together like water, ships, and sailors. It's a learning process that all men go through until they develop control. It's usually a painful development."

"That's the truth," John muttered." I wasted loads of yen, before I learnt my lessons. In the States, I was even worse. Made a damn fool outta myself with every woman I tried to get on first base with." John yawned. "Live and learn. Kimiko has taught me more about life than I ever learnt in school or back home. God, I love her."

Tim perked up. "Really, John? Do you love her?"

John hung his big head. "Yeah, but she won't marry me. Says she'll never leave Japan, and she helps her mother out. Her brother too, sends them money all the time. Her older brother is starting some business, televisions, radios, things like that; she's helping him get started." A somber look came over John's face.

"The Marine Corps not gonna let me stay here forever. I'm thinking about re-enlisting, I get discharged in July." He looked at Tim. "Fast four years, huh, Tim?"

"Not for me, John, I can't wait to get out and go back home, I'm counting the days, one hundred and two, counting today."

John took a drink and lit one of Tim's cigarettes. Tim lit one too, his other having burned away in the ashtray. "I gotta make up my mind soon; I'm scheduled to rotate back home next month. I've been here over two years. It feels like home to me. If I reenlist for three, till '63, the Corps will let me stay here two more years. I'll be twenty five then, not exactly an old man."

"Why stay, John? If Kimiko won't marry you, you'll only be putting off the inevitable. Unless you think she'll change her mind with more time."

John took a big drink and sighed. "That's what I'm thinking, hoping, I guess."

They sat in silence drinking and smoking. Tim felt John's pain. He also made a decision, a wrong one as it turned out. In high school, he'd gone steady with Sarah from the tenth grade. Never in his mind did he think he'd lose her to another guy, but he did, all because of a wrong decision. After graduating from high school, instead of waiting to be drafted into the Army, he joined the Navy to see some of the world, and at the same time get his obligated military service behind him. In his young blank mind, he'd thought she would wait for him forever. In his young blank mind, Sarah wouldn't even think of kissing another man. In his young blank mind, they'd both be virgins until their honeymoon. In his young blank mind they were doing the right thing by waiting to have sex and God would bless them for living by his rules. With his young blank mind, he almost jumped overboard when he got her Dear John letter in the middle of the Pacific Ocean. John broke the silence.

"You know I named that bar, Harrigan's?"

Tim smiled. "How did that come about?"

"The owner, a tall guy for Japanese, wanted to be a doctor, but the war screwed up his plans. So after the war, he opened a bar, then another, then another. I don't know how many he owns. I call him Ben Casey, after the TV doctor. Anyhow, when he was opening Harrigan's, being I was such a good customer of his, he asked me to give the new bar a name, he wanted an Irish name. I couldn't think of any name but Harrigan's that I'd be sure of spelling right. You know me, Tim, never was too good with readin' and writin,' but I remembered that play in high school that you and Bonnie were great in, singing and dancing together. I was in the chorus, in the background, but we practiced singing that Harrigan song so many times I never forgot it. We had to sing out each letter in the name Harrigan. Remember? Ben Casey loves the name. And I'm here to tell you it's brought him a lot of yen."

Tim stretched out on the floor. "How can you afford this place?"

"It takes everything I got Tim, and Kimiko helps out." John followed Tim onto the floor, stretching his muscular frame over the mats. "Do you get many letters from home, Tim?"

"Just my parents."

"None from Sarah?"

Tim answered matter of fact. "She got married, John. Not to me."

John didn't answer, but was shocked and was glad Tim couldn't see his face. After a moment he spoke. "I never get any letters. Who would write me? My Dad is dead. Who? My Mother and her boyfriend? I wish I had some brothers and sisters. Don't you, Tim?"

Tim was thinking of his lost love, but forced an answer. "Sometimes."

On their backs, staring at the ceiling, feeling the whiskey taking a hold on their minds, the friends lay having deep painful thoughts of women in their lives that caused them suffering. When John spoke, it was his turn to shock Tim. "You know, Tim, my mother was making love to her boyfriend before Dad died. I loved my Dad. While Dad was in his bedroom dying, my mother was making love to that jerk she goes with on our living room sofa. I walked in on them after school. I was in the eighth grade. Let me tell you, that's a hellava way to see yer mother!"

Tim changed the subject. "Who were those kids outside?" Then laughed hard. "Yours?"

John chuckled. "No, but I wish they were. I like kids. Their parents own this house. They live on the other side, more in back of the house. The whole place is nuttin' but a bunch of sliding doors. They never bother us, even when I'm having a party. These people are too damn polite. But we pay our rent on time and I bring them gifts from the base."

Tim yawned. He was getting sleepy. John rolled onto his stomach and pointed to a wall. "Over there is our bedroom, and over, there." He pointed further along the same wall. "It's our guest room with a bed. I can't sleep on the floor like the Japanese do, and I don't expect my guests to either. Maybe, if you're lucky Tim-san, sailor boy, sea dog, maybe Kimiko will feel sorry for you tonight and bring home a friend to keep you warm."

Tim became alert. "Do you think she will?"

"With Kimiko, one never knows. She could bring home two for a sailor she liked, who was at sea so long! What the hell do you do with yourself aboard ship in your spare time?"

"Read."

"God, I'm glad I didn't join the Navy. And speaking of God, Tim, Mama-san, behind the house, has a big statue of Buddha. She prays all the time. I mean all these Gods, who the hell knows, all these religions? I don't believe in God. Not since the day I saw my mother on the sofa grinning at me like a child caught with her hand in the cookie jar. What kinda God would let a young boy see such a thing, and with Dad dying in the next room, giving off the death rattle?" John kept talking about his mother, but Tim wasn't listening.

Tim understood John's confusion about God. Even before joining the Navy, he had long thoughts about life. And since joining the Navy, the awful sights he witnessed in some port calls in the Orient. The harshness of life some people endured. A missionary came to his ship once and begged for some food. Some vegetables that were turning bad were given to him and the priest scurried away from the dock pulling his cart full of rotting vegetables, happy as a clown at a birthday party. John quit talking. Soon they were both asleep.

"Reveille sailor! It's time to party!" John was calling him.

"Wake up, Tim-san." Kimiko was shaking him. He sat up. Kimiko was smiling at him. John was filling glasses with ice and whiskey. Other Japanese people were in the room. Tim found himself grinning at strangers. John handed him a drink. Ben Casey in suit and tie was shaking his hand, introducing him to some other women and men. Kimiko sat beside him. She looked sober enough. She was chattering rapidly with two other pretty girls also wearing slit satin dresses. Tim took big gulps from his drink.

Kimiko turned to Tim. "John-san use much whiskey."

"Takusan whiskey!" Tim shouted over the other voices.

"You remember takusan." Kimiko smiled, pleased that he remember the word she taught him. "You and John-san have good time today?"

Tim nodded. "My tomodachi."

"Very good." she said and took his hand.

Tim liked holding her hand but felt awkward doing it with John in the room. The other guests laughed and talked among themselves. It was rare if Tim or Kimiko got interrupted in their own conversation.

The suit and tie dressed bartenders and the scantily adorned women were drinking heavily and enjoying John's antics. Ben Casey had a camera and a cloth bag full of flash bulbs, burning them off as he circled the room. The party lasted well into the morning. Kimiko gave Tim lessons in Japanese while John and the others sang and danced around the room. They danced some sort of traditional Japanese dance with a lot of body bending and waving of arms. By the time most of the guests left, Tim was drunk and John was passed out on the floor, his kimono opened to his big hairy chest. Kimiko took Tim to the guest room and laid him down on the bed and undressed him. Kimiko was whispering to him and slithering out of her satin. Ben Casey was packing up his things, but still got off more flashes before stumbling outside. Tim didn't speak. He didn't question her or his betrayal of John. He didn't question anything. The only thing he wanted to do and did was roll Kimiko onto the bed and make love to her.

When Tim and his hangover awoke in late afternoon, the only evidence that Kimiko has shared his bed was a long strand of black hair, lost and alone, and draped over the white pillow. He dreaded facing John who he could hear moving about behind the paper sliding door. He gathered the bravado necessary, got up out of the comfortable bed, dressed, and slid open the door.

John, looking bright and relaxed, sitting crossed-legged aside the varnished table, poured Tim a cup of hot green tea and handed it to him. Tim, whose throat was sore from smoking and drinking, mumbled something to his friend, which was supposed to pass off as thanks. He didn't look at John directly, casting his eyes to the side. To his relief, through the open door to John's bedroom, he could see Kimiko in a white kimono sound asleep in John's bed.

If John suspected or knew of Kimiko's unfaithfulness with his friend, he never revealed it in his actions or words towards Tim. Tim sipped his tea feeling guilty, but in his heart he knew he was a different man since losing Sarah. He knew he would most likely do Kimiko again and again if given the chance. That grimy realization about himself did not please him.

CHAPTER THREE

The dance hall was a dark place. The overhead lights dimmed down to a mellow glow. The brightest light came from a colorful jukebox in the corner near where Tim and Orson sat. They were alone in the big room sipping Iron City Beer out of brown bottles and smoking cigarettes. Orson was cheery, full of confidence in his sexual prowess. Tim had the jitters.

Noise floated into the dance hall from other locations inside the Rivers Bend Social Club. Young masculine voices came from the crowded bar, conveniently positioned between the dance floor and bowling lanes. The crashing sound of shattering tenpins mixed with feminine shrills drifted to the waiting men, stirring their minds with lustful expectancy.

It was a summer evening in Rivers Bend and women's bowling night at the Social Club, followed by dancing. It was the source of shrills that brought the young steel workers to the club every Friday night, being willingly herded there by unruly hormones. It was those same shrills that filled Orson with sexual expectation and Tim with anxiety. Especially Sarah's shrill. Orson was talking.

"At least you didn't marry before goin' into the Navy, like dummy me."

"Do you ever hear from your ex?" Tim asked.

"Nope," Orson snarled. "I think she's near St. Louis. That's where my Dear John was postmarked." Orson wiped some beer foam from his lips with the back of his hand but kept on talking. "Of course, she could have mailed it to me from a motel on a stop over screw with that steel hauler she took off with. Her family won't tell me where she's at, not that I want her back. I'd just like to write her a letter, tell her how her goin' was the best thing that ever happened to me. Nothing but one-nighters for me from now on."

Tim kept quiet while Orson revealed himself and his anger. Tim wondered how the others he would see tonight might have also changed. Four years was a long time to be away from home and he expected changes in the lives of his hometown friends. But Orson's anger and bitterness surprised him and made him feel uncomfortable sitting and listening like an altar boy while being lectured to about women. In Orson's world you shouldn't ever give them anything 'cept a penis and contempt. Tim lowered his eyes to the table and fidgeted with his beer bottle.

His own experience with heartache after receiving Sarah's Dear John was crushing pain. Getting through his duties aboard ship was a torturous task and when he was relieved from his duties, he ran to his bunk and remained there as long as possible. Taking a shower was a task, all conversation from his shipmates was bothersome and unwelcome. Food was disgusting. Coffee and cigarette smoke was all he cared to subsist on during his watch topside on the open deck until that diet made him physically sick. He was sent to sick bay where slowly he regained his appetite. In time, other thoughts besides Sarah shared his mind and he learned to survive from day to day without the assurance of a sunny future.

Orson was talking about Sarah and Tim's eyes opened wider. He sat up erect and alert in his wooden chair.

"She bowls and dances some, mostly with other women. I never saw her leave the club with a pick up."

Tim was glad to hear that account from Orson, but not the next one out of his mouth.

"She should be getting horny, Tim." Orson sneered. "You came home just in time!"

Tim didn't answer Orson's crude remark, only grimaced. He felt it was going to be a long night of awkwardness with Sarah at the club and an angry friend in denial of his continuing love for the wife that jilted him. He wanted to know more.

"Did you ever meet her husband?" Tim queried.

"Once." Orson turned his head from Tim and blew smoke from his mouth. "Here at the club. He's a salesman in restaurant supplies. That's how he met Sarah. She's back, by the way, working at the Steak and Ale House again. Claims she can make more money as a waitress than working in some office. I gotta give her credit, she's got her own place, an apartment. In fact, on my first day home from the Navy, the whole gang helped move her from her mother's house. It's a nice apartment, but it's on the third floor. Thank God she didn't have too much heavy stuff to carry up those steps. Most of her furniture and appliances are furnished. I was thinking of getting a furnished place myself. I gotta get my own place. Living with my parents is bad for my love life. Motels are too expensive and you have to be out by eleven in the morning. Christ, sometimes on the weekends, I'm only getting a babe into bed a few hours earlier than that and then it's time to get up and go." Orson chuckled to himself. "Hardly enough time for seconds!"

Tim wanted him to talk about Sarah. Not himself.

"Anyhow," Orson paused, "Her husband liked to bullshit, slap you on the back type guy. A showoff. He was older than us, five years older, I'd guess. Dressed loud, wearing the brightest damn yellow tie. Called it his neon tie. They lived East of Pittsburgh, well at least she did and she said he was never at home. They seemed happy enough the night they were here. They left arm and arm. The jackass gave me a "V" for victory salute when he was leaving. Like who couldn't make out with their own wife...are you going for her tonight?"

"Christ, Orson!" Tim got unsettled hearing about Sarah's marriage and becoming peeved that she ditched him for a boaster, a loudmouth. "I just got discharged. Didn't you feel somewhat nervous, apprehensive, when you got out of the Navy, away from all that regimentation! I'm just glad to be home, slowly adjusting. Had I known Sarah was going to be here tonight, I might not have even come to the Club."

"Take it easy, Tim. Calm down, you'll adjust to freedom. By the way, Sarah has a baby. A girl, about two years old."

Tim had never been told that Sarah had had a baby. It shocked him. Sarah had a baby girl. She was a mother! It didn't seem possible.

Orson smiled. "She knows you're here. When I went to the restroom earlier I ran into her. Her mouth dropped open."

"That's probably a good thing," Tim rushed the words out of his mouth. "Now, she'll probably dash home after bowling."

"Tim, wake up, she's coming to the dance. Do you think those women really come here to bowl? Crap man, this is 1960, they come to flirt. Married, divorced, separated, single, they all come for the same reason. To get the hell outta the house, to be teased, charmed, and made to feel wanted. They're pussycats Tim. Remember that and you'll be okay. Bowling is just their way of meowing, 'I'm bored, open the door, I'm going out.' Orson's hazel eyes sparkled. "If they happened to run into an ally cat like me, they meow. It wasn't planned, it just happened. Virgins aren't bowling tonight, Tim. The virgins are walking' hand in hand through City Park with their sweethearts, dreaming of how nice it'll be when they marry and get to sleep together every night."

Tim changed the conversation. "Who else will be here tonight?"

"Fitch for sure. And his wife, Gypsy. She's in there bowling now with Sarah. Wait till you meet her. She shits all over Fitch."

"Where is she from?"

"Pittsburgh. She worked with Bonnie in Pittsburgh. Bonnie brought her around a few years ago and Fitch scooped her. Then she got knocked up and they hitched. But it's a marriage made in hell. They have two kids." Orson got a grin on his face and leaned across the table and whispered, even though they were still alone in the big room.

"Don't say anything, but I had her." Orson straightened his muscular body and lifted his bottle of beer and smiled triumphantly at Tim. "It's great. I get a rush every time I see Fitch. It's like knowing Fitch's best kept secret."

Orson's confession of betraying their friend Fitch forced thoughts of John into Tim's mind and his own weakness for the flesh of a woman. That allowed him to enjoy Kimiko's pleasures with John passed out only a few meters away. He'd be the last to scold Orson.

"You know John re-enlisted for three more years? He has a Japanese girlfriend. I met her. She's very beautiful, smart."

"Smarter than my cousin, re-enlisting, he must've lost his mind." Orson stood up and looked toward the bowling alley. "They'll be coming soon. I'm going to get us some refills."

Tim offered to buy the beers.

"Hey," Orson chuckled. "It's on me. I remember what Navy pay was like. Yesterday was payday at the mill, I'm loaded." Orson took off in a quick step across the hardwood floor. He had an athletic swaggering gait, a conqueror's fancy in his moves. It was all a game to Orson, and the dance floor the arena.

They were no longer alone in the dance hall. The wooden tables surrounding the dancing floor were beginning to be taken by men coming from the bar. Men in groups and men alone, all are waiting, and sipping, and hoping, like deer hunters in a tree stand hoping to snag a doe passing by.

His new life was just beginning and Tim was already despondent, not at all like he thought he would feel after leaving the Navy. He thought being home would be about the same as it was before, except for the hole Sarah left in his life, but otherwise pretty much the same as before. The atmosphere of the Social Club was different. The club didn't feel like a family place anymore, not like he recalled it while growing up in the forties and fifties. Many times he came to the club with his parents and joined up with other neighborhood boys. They drank sodas and played games while their folks, dressed in their Sunday best, socialized. Without children or families, the club seemed no different than an ordinary tavern. Tim looked around the dance floor. Except for a few older men wearing a suit and tie, most like Orson wore a colorful pullover and tight blue jeans. Tim, in his white short sleeve shirt and pressed khaki pants felt dressed for a high school history class. Orson returned with their beers.

"They're done bowling, changing shoes, dolling themselves up for us." Orson sat down hard. Spotted Fitch and Dutch entering the hall. "Fitch, over here!" He yelled across the floor.

Tim felt better just seeing two buddies approaching. Each was carrying a bottle of beer. They looked about the same to Tim, but Dutch had gained weight and his pullover stretched against his expanding belly. "Well," Tim thought, "at least they're clean shaven and well-scrubbed." He stood up to greet his pals. He barely finished shaking Fitch and Dutch's hands and exchanging a few teasing comments when Orson gave out the alert in a loud yelp. "Here they come!"

Tim looked at the elated Orson. He was gazing at the women entering the dance hall in bunches, appearing to Tim much like a caged bull about to be turned loose on a herd of prized cows. Soon the hall was vibrating with noise. Voices got louder, tables were being pushed together, and chairs rationed out. Tim watched for Sarah. His heart began beating fast, too fast. He sat down, took a long drink of cold beer, and sighed. This evening was going to be a nightmare to remember.

Music came from the jukebox that raised his spirits. It was soft, it was gentle, and it was Sinatra. Colorful track lighting was turned on, sending their shafts of light to a rotating shiny ball hanging from the ceiling. Couples were embracing on the dance floor.

A woman was beside Tim, being introduced to him. He collected his thoughts and stood up. Fitch was talking to him. "Brogan, this is my wife, Gypsy. Gypsy, the one and only Tim Brogan, the best song and dance man Rivers Bend High ever graduated." Tim took her extended hand. "Don't believe him, Gypsy. I'm glad to meet you."

Gypsy's big full lips opened and locked into a permanent flashing smile. "Hmm," she murmured, "after that introduction, I guess I'll need to try you out." Her face glowed around big brown eyes. "On the dance floor, that is."

After what Orson had revealed about Gypsy, Tim stayed cautious with his response. "If Fitch doesn't mind."

Gypsy took her hand from Tim's and stroked it along his cheek. "He won't mind, honey." Tim sat down and handled his beer bottle. Gypsy leaned close to him, her short wavy brown hair clinging to her head like feathers, they were nose to nose and Tim didn't know what to say. "Make it soon, handsome," she whispered. "A fast dance please." Tim could smell her breath, almost taste the spearmint exhaled on him. To Brogan's relief she stood and sat down in the chair across the table between her husband and Orson.

Others joined around, pushing tables together. Tim still didn't know if Sarah was in the dance hall, and he didn't want to stand and gawk in the faintness to see where she was sitting. He desperately hoped someone; anyone would mention her name, where she was at in the room, or if she'd left the club. Ironically, it was the friend long ago noted for being thrifty with both money and words that mentioned her name first.

"Who's Sarah sitting with over there? Why isn't she sitting here with us?" Not everyone at the table looked at Dutch for bringing up Sarah's name. Tim didn't, but those that did made funny faces at Dutch that could have easily spelled out ouch. But not Gypsy.

"She's afraid to face Tim."

The table went silent. A fast song blared from the jukebox, and Gypsy leaped to her feet and rushed to Tim and grabbed him with both hands. Tim followed Gypsy to a dancing area in full view of Sarah's table. She had her back to him and Tim thought Sarah purposely positioned her face away from where he sat.

Tim took Gypsy into his arms, picked up the beat of the music and moved her about gracefully. Gypsy's white tight slacks promised a man smooth firm fun, and her large breasts, unrestrained by a brassiere, moved with ease beneath her pink halter. But Tim's mind would have none of Gypsy's charm; it was fixed only on Sarah's back, and her dark brown shoulder length hair, cut shorter since their days together. Mercifully for Tim, the music stopped. Gypsy came to him spinning into his arms, giggling. "Oh, Timmy honey, we've got to do this again." Without comment he got her back to her husband.

The conversation went on around Tim. People got up and left the table, people came back and sat at the table, people laughed, people giggled, people patted him on the back and welcomed him back home. But Tim's brain was hardly functioning to the happenings around him. He smiled, nodded, smoked and drank from the beer bottles, unaware of what he did from one moment to the next. He was only alert to Sarah's back. The beer kept coming, and full bottles of brew were bunching up untouched in front of him. In his state of mind, he wasn't mindful that he wasn't keeping up with the others. Again Dutch pointed this fault out to him.

"Holy hell, Tim, you forget how to drink in the Navy."

Tim gave off a weak smile. "I can't keep up with you steelworkers, so please don't buy me anymore." Tim pushed some of the full bottles to the others around the table. Sarah was driving him crazy. He couldn't leave tonight without at least talking to her. His heart was full of fear because he knew the truth. It jumped right into his face on the dance floor with Gypsy. Gypsy was as well proportioned and sexy as any woman the average guy meets, yet with all of her twisting and turning and humping and bouncing boobs, not one watt of excitement charged through his body. Yet the simple thought of crossing over to where Sarah sat and touching her hair became a far greater desirable goal for him than dreaming of scoring with Gypsy. He still loved Sarah but feared what all men fear. Being made the chump. Sarah could have him back this very night, but he could never trust her again. Being a chump once was painful enough, being a chump twice, much better to walk the Rivers Bend Bridge and jump into the Ohio with a placard round your neck. "Once Sarah's chump, always Sarah's chump." Someone was shouting his name. He recognized the voice. It was Bonnie and she was rushing towards him. He stood and took her into his arms.

"Timothy!" She sang out in the same clear voice Brogan remembered so well.

Tim held her at arms length, studying her. She was still extremely thin, a cardboard cutout figure. "God, I missed you!" he said. "I thought of you often while I was away."

She smiled parting her thin lips. She wore no makeup. "Sure you did. That's why I got two letters in four years."

"I did, honest." Tim chuckled. Bonnie brought him out of his dark mood. He was genuinely smiling, not forcing it as with the others. "How could I ever forget our song and dance routines at school? You were great, Bonnie."

"Ahhh, go on. You held me together, and I loved it."

Tim turned her tall thin body around. She looked taller to him, and he thought perhaps it was the dark slacks. She wore a pale green blouse and was nearly flat in front. "You haven't aged a bit, Bonnie. You look the same."

"I know!" she snapped. "That's why I can't get a man. Didn't find any magic potions on those exotic islands you visited, the kind that turn Plain Jane into Plentiful Jane?"

Brogan shook his head. "Still beating up on yourself, I see."

"Habit!"

Tim pulled at her arm. "Come on, sit down with me."

She came close to Tim and whispered into his ear. "Friendships aren't as they were, Tim. Things change dear." She kissed him on the cheek. Orson saw her kiss.

"All right, Bonnie!" Orson yelped. "Go for it!" Bonnie tossed him a look of displeasure.

"Ohh, excuse me," Orson mocked.

"Orson, you're drunk!" Bonnie snapped. "You can be such an asshole!"

Orson sneered. "I remember a night when you didn't think so!" Some men at the table snickered.

Fire came into Bonnie's eyes. "Even then I did, Orson! Believe me!"

Tim, still holding Bonnie's hands, was stunned by this fighting amongst his old friends. "I'm sitting by the fire exit, Tim, with some friends from Pittsburgh, stop over before the night is over." She kissed him on the cheek and walked away.

Tim had enough of Orson. "Orson, what the hell is with you? Bonnie's an old friend."

"What?" Orson drank from his bottle.

Tim let the moment pass. "Nothing." He sat back down. Orson's hint that he'd slept with Bonnie didn't surprise him. Many men did.

Gypsy asked him to dance but he turned her down. She went off to the dance floor arm in arm with Orson. Dutch and Fitch and a few others were talking about the Pirates, how good they were playing and the possibility of a World Series in Pittsburgh. Something none of them ever experienced as long as they lived in the Western Pennsylvanian hills around Pittsburgh.

It was getting late, Tim looked over at Sarah's table, and someone was asking her to dance. She refused the man without turning around in her chair. Now somebody else was talking to him, a bulky red headed man, a well groomed stranger. "I'm sorry," Tim apologized. "I didn't see you sit down." Tim noticed the man's right arm was shorter than his left, his hand reduced in size.

"I said do you want a job?" Tim was still in a haze of confusion about himself, Sarah, and his friends.

"Job?" Tim questioned.

"Ben is the name." Ben didn't offer his good left hand to shake. "I own a bar. The Piano Bar across the river. Do you want work playing piano? Bonnie tells me you're very good, very talented."

"You're a friend of Bonnie's?"

"She visits my place often."

"Playing piano?" Tim asked.

Ben smiled at Tim's stupid look. "Yeah, what else?"

"Ahh, thanks Ben, but right now I'm not sure what I want. I might go to college."

"Good enough," Ben answered, stood and patted Tim's shoulder. "If school doesn't work out, give me a holler." Ben turned and walked away. Tim followed him with his eyes to Bonnie's table. If he went to college, closing a bar at two in the morning wouldn't be very favorable to studying. He sat back down and faked interest in the sport talk going on heatedly around the table.

Playing piano for a wage would be great. Easy sing along stuff. Seldom aboard ship did he have any pleasure, but on those occasions, when for some reason or another, he was asked to play for the crew, he enjoyed himself. Particularly at Christmastime, when the call for his talent was daily. The sailors would come into the recreation room, gather around the upright, sing carols, making themselves feel both happy and more homesick at the same time. He got pleasure from their pleasure and found out a bit more about himself. He liked helping people.

Tim looked around. Gypsy was standing behind Orson's chair, her hands down inside of his shirt, rubbing her hands over his chest. Fitch was talking to Dutch and the others about his job at the mill, acting nonchalant about his wife's behavior. Fitch looked tired. He never grew tall, the smallest of the gang. In a lot of ways he still looked like a teenager, but his eyes looked tired to Brogan, and his mind far away.

Tim looked again towards Sarah's table. His heart jumped inside his chest. The chair was empty. She wasn't sitting there! He panicked. What did he do to himself? How did he allow her to go home without any contact? The booze loosened his fear. He had to find out where she went. He got up and walked to where Sarah had been sitting. Before he got that far, she appeared from the short passageway to the rest rooms. They caught each other's eye and neither had the desire or ability to turn their heads away. They walked directly into each other's arms, onto the dance floor and just held each other, scarcely moving to the song, *Only You*, being harmonized by the Platters.

CHAPTER FOUR

Briefly in the spring, the beautiful and aromatic lilac bushes in the city park burst forth with a strong pleasing scent that no other foliage can overwhelm. The smell given off by the blooming bushes growing in abundance around the boundaries of the park carried quite a distance. Sarah's apartment building was near the west end of the oblong park, and whiffs of the sweet smell drifted through the open windows during those glorious few weeks of spring when the lilac blossoms bloom.

It was a bright sunny morning and Sarah was as if she could not get enough of the flowery smell. She was still in her nightgown, without makeup and had her dark hair bunched up on top of her head while leaning through the wide open kitchen window. On tiptoes, she stretched her body to its limits while taking deep breaths of the outside air, inhaling and exhaling and delighting in the beautiful morning. Tim stood behind her softly holding onto her shapely hips. When she came back inside, he cuddled her. She pressed herself against him and methodically rotated her hips until she felt him becoming aroused.

"I love you and the smell of lilac," she whispered close into his ear.

Tim smiled. "Be thankful the steel barons built the mill on the east end of town or else you'd be smelling less lilac and more industry."

Sarah chuckled. "This is a perfect morning for me. Lynn is still fast asleep, the sun is shining, lilacs are blooming, and my lover stopped in to see me on his way to work. And he's wearing his dark brown suit, which makes him look even more handsome than his other suits."

Tim held her at arm length. "What was that?" he laughed. "A compliment for me or a billboard for the color brown."

Sarah twisted out of his grasp giggling. "Get to work, big boy, and take that new growth inside your pants with you." She chuckled louder. "I'm feeling threatened."

"You are?" He started loosening his light green colored tie and whispered harshly, "And you have every right to be!" Tim chased after her into the bedroom." I'm a salesman, remember? We have no regular work hours."

Sarah fell onto her back across the bed smiling. "Ohhh salesman, I have no money, do you have free samples?"

Tim was scattering his clothes over the carpet floor in his haste to undress and get onto the bed with Sarah. "Upon request?" Tim stood naked over her.

"I request, I request, I urgently request," Sarah sang out and reached out for him. Brogan went on top of and into her beauty.

After they finished making love, Tim rushed around the bedroom gathering up his clothes, and then headed towards the bathroom. Sarah lowered her gown but stayed lying across the bed. She called after him. "Tim, for our sanity, won't you please move in with me? This leaving late at night, then showing up first thing in the morning is crazy. Wouldn't it be wonderful being in bed together every night?" She waited for his response but none came from the bathroom. The only sound she heard was Lynn calling out for her from the small back bedroom.

Scrubbing his hands over the small sink, Tim thought he should move in with Sarah. He desperately wanted to be with her every possible moment his life would allow. But he was having troubles, a mental dilemma that she knew nothing of, nor did he feel comfortable speaking to her about this newly discovered problem.

He looked at himself in the mirror over the sink. His full head of sandy hair was wavy. Since being discharged from the Navy nine months earlier, he'd let his hair grow out. He ran his fingers through it to fluff it up. His light blue eyes sparkled. He straightened his tie. "Soon Sarah, I promise," he hollered out to her. Then he lied to her. "I told you before, as soon as I feel secure in my sales, making enough money, this will be my address." He straightened himself up and walked to Sarah who was feeding Lynn in the kitchen. They kissed lightly and Tim rushed out the door yelling over his shoulder, "I'll see you tonight."

Tim sat inside of his small car but did not start the motor. He thought about his problem, the thoughts he was having about Sarah and her husband. Jealous thoughts. Wondering if she ever did this or that with her husband like she did with him. Not only annoying thoughts over the larger intimate familiarities that are shared by lovers, but little everyday things. Like did he ever hold onto her hips as she bent to smell flowers, or reach over and touch her hand while dining? He worried that the distasteful and unwanted thoughts would get worse and more frequent if he moved in with her.

He never thought of himself as a jealous man, never would expect a man to be jealous over a woman's failed first marriage. Every human makes mistakes. But he was jealous, was resentful, and felt very offended by Sarah and he understood why. He wasn't coming into her life as someone new, someone untouched by her hurtful rejection. She had broken her word to him, her promise to wait for him and remain virtuous. He had promised her that he could and would do the same for her. No amount of temptation could have made him break that promise.

He felt cheated for not experiencing her first, for not living with her first. He rubbed his face hard. He was driving himself crazy. Now he wished he'd never have known Sarah before enlisting into the Navy and would have only recently met her since being discharged. His mind could handle being in her future without ever having been in her past.

"Quit whining and be grateful for what you got." he mumbled to himself, lit a cigarette, started the motor and drove off to work just as a new distressful thought popped into his brain. Her husband was a salesman, too, with no fixed work hours, leaving him as well with plenty of time for morning play.

CHAPTER FIVE

Since that summer night at the Social Club now over two years ago when Tim and Sarah had come together on the dance floor, they had gone to Pittsburgh as often as they could fit the short trip into their budget. They went to musicals at Heinz Hall and The Benedum Center, leisurely walked the Carnegie Museum, held hands through a Pittsburgh Symphony performance, took a cruise up and down Pittsburgh's three rivers and enjoyed the zoo and aviary many times.

Sarah loved the flower shows at Phipps, and just preferred to see anything with animals or plants instead of sporting events. They did attend one Penguin hockey game, and several Pirate baseball games, but she favored the zoo and the antics of animals over humans.

Other than their one-day excursions to Pittsburgh, they chose to remain at Sarah's apartment and had not gone to the Social Club since the night of their resurrected affection. For a while they were called and pestered by the group to come out to the Club, but even Gypsy's persistence for Sarah to keep bowling with her faded. At last they were left pretty much to themselves, bathing in their ecstasy of love and rejoicing in the simple of the simplest things in life. Cuddling one another on strolls through the city park, writing messages to each other in a new snow, or just staring into each others eyes by the radiance of a bright moon was time too thrilling and precious to be discarded for bowling balls and beer.

Tim finally thought he had gotten his negative thoughts against Sarah's past rejection of him under control and moved in with Sarah and her little girl. Together they did all the things young couples do just as if they were man and wife, but they avoided talk of marriage even though Sarah's divorce became final. Sleeping together night after night and waking up each morning with Sarah in his arms was the highlight of each day for Tim.

That first night, after leaving the Social Club together, they rushed to her apartment arm in arm. Then Tim, after fantasizing and longing an eternity, felt like Adam discovering Eve and was as full of thankfulness as the first man had to be when given by God the gift for the source of life. Loneliness, brooding, and boredom passed from his being and he was without resentful thoughts for a time.

Sarah kept her job at the Steak and Ale House, working both the lunch and early dinner shifts. Sarah's mother would babysit Lynn until

Tim picked her up in late afternoon. The child turned four and was curious about anything bright and noisy. She was a joy to Tim and he loved the little girl.

Brogan passed on college and took a job as a salesman with a paint manufacturing company. He did well, but earned far less than a steelworker and sometimes money was hard to find between the both of them after the bills were paid. However, Tim liked his job and got to travel around the tri-state region of Pennsylvania, Ohio, and West Virginia, meeting people and listening to music as he drove a company car from place to place.

Because of his sales record being worthy and obtaining a high aptitude score on a linguistic test given by the company, he was being tutored along with several other salesmen in Spanish, which pleased his restless mind. The company had plans to expand to an international level, beginning south of the border. Singing Latin Mass with the Saint James Boys Choir while attending grade school, and later with the men's choir until he joined the Navy, Tim believed, gave him an edge on the test.

After a while, when their lives settled into a daily routine of touching and kissing and caring, the reality of life would prick at their love bubble with questions that sooner or later had to be asked and answered about their future. That was when his envious thoughts returned and began lingering too long in his brain. Thoughts of Sarah and her former husband, sprinkled mind's eye views from the two of them making love to eating breakfast together.

He hid those thoughts from her, smothering his jealousy with what he knew to be certain. Sarah loved him. He was glad he never saw her husband or even a picture of him. He was always a murky man in his mind, but he never forgot what Orson had said about him, that he was a show off type of a guy who talked a lot and wore loud colored clothes. But even armed with Sarah's love, glimpses of unwanted impression of her married life still could not be stopped, only overcome, and Brogan pushed himself to override the unwelcome intrusions into his mind with happy thoughts of the two of them enjoying their lives together.

He worried for his mental health and did not want to become as sick and out of bounds as he'd experienced aboard ship, but the reel of images of Sarah and the murky man in his mind's eye kept turning and turning. But unlike a bad movie, the end never comes, and there was no walking out for Tim on his own private show.

The sun was turning down after a hot August day. Tim, only in shorts and laying on his back across their bed, felt refreshed against the heat of the day studying his Spanish and listening to a Peggy Lee long playing record. Their bedroom and Lynn's were air conditioned, but the rest of the apartment remained hot and humid. Lynn was sleeping soundly. Earlier the three of them had gone to the public swimming pool and the watery afternoon had exhausted the child.

Sarah was in the shower. Something was bothering her, but whatever it was she wasn't talking to Tim about it. She'd been dull all day. At the pool, she went through the motions of splashing fun in a weak manner, most unlike the perky Sarah he loved. Tim heard the shower stop and the hair dryer start. "Pájaro raro" he murmured.

Sarah was a sort of a rare bird. Beautiful in face and figure. Graceful in a wholesome body. Her penetrating green eyes always caused considerable notice by people that came into contact with her. And her thick brown hair was always a joy to touch. She had a quick wit and a natural intelligence about her, but she wasn't scholarly or much interested in reading beyond the daily newspaper and magazines. They did have one common trait; neither was much interested in television, contented to fill their apartment with music.

On occasion, she would convince herself that she was holding him back in life, that he would be better fulfilled if he went to college and entered the business world with a degree. She always marveled at the stored up knowledge he filled his brain with by reading books on philosophy, psychology, theology, and history.

He had cardboard boxes full of books he had read stored both at the apartment and at his parent's house. He found it more than difficult to toss or give a book away. It was almost sinful to him. He couldn't help himself. He loved learning. And unknown to Sarah, his plunge into heavy reading began in the Navy after he recovered from his depressing disorder brought about by her marriage vows to Mr. Murky.

In his own mind he remained true and steadfast to the character of the Tim he himself liked. The Tim seeing and grieving over Sarah and Mr. Murky he did not like. That up front normalcy frightened Brogan somewhat because he knew genuine scary madmen all come across as normal nice guys. The hair dryer stopped its whining and soon Sarah came into the cool room dressed only in a knee-length cloth robe which was tied tightly around her waist. She lay down close to Tim. Her curls brushed against his cheek and it sent a yearning through his body. He could envision her nakedness beneath the robe. Her clean sweet scent came to his nostrils. He dropped his book over the side of the bed to the floor and turned to her. He kissed her full

lips lightly, ran his hand over her bunched up hair and onto her exposed shapely neck. She turned his advances away by rolling a full turn of her body across the bed and sat cross legged, propping her head up with her elbows. She looked at him with darkened eyes. She was studying him.

Tim chuckled. "What's this? Rejection? Is there something I should know? Am I growing horns, a tail perhaps?"

"Tim, we have to talk. About us."

Tim laid the back of his head down on the pillow and stared up at the ceiling. "Go on."

Sarah swung her feet off the bed, stood up, and pulled the plug on Peggy Lee. When the music died, the room became hushed and Tim could hear her robe moving against her flesh as she walked in front of him to her side of the bed. She sat on the bed and faced him.

"Tim," she paused. "Lynn is getting older. Is it good for her, growing up with us living in our present state?"

Tim laughed. "What's this? A proposal?"

Sarah gave off a weak smile. "Please Tim, let me finish. I was married in the church. You know that and sometimes I think perhaps that's the reason, and I hope the only reason you never talk about marrying me. I don't feel comfortable bringing up my divorce with you because," she paused again. "Well, because of my past behavior towards you, ditching you for a jerk. And since my ex-jerk has never and will never send support money for Lynn, marrying me will place financial and parental responsibilities on you that someday might make you feel unfairly put upon."

Tim laid limp showing no spark to what she had said so far, so she continued. "I love you to the pit of my being, but I would rather live without you before living with you in a state of remorse for taking me back into your life." She turned away from him.

Tim closed his eyes tight and questioned himself. She had picked up on his increasing silent spells and had questioned him about it briefly before. He had waved those quiet moods off to her as only silent quiz Spanish conversation being held with himself. He believed that she didn't have a trace that his depression over Mr. Murky was becoming more serious. Tidbits of his jealousy must've shown through the ordinary Tim. He opened his eyes and was grateful for her expressed love for him. It lifted his spirits and was like adding ammunition to his arsenal in his battle with Mr. Murky. "Is that all this is about? Getting married, taking care of little Lynn? I don't see a future for me without you and Lynn in it."

Sarah moved further on the bed and leaned her back against the headboard. She still looked somber. "What about the church? The Catholic way was a big part of your life before we came back together."

Tim closed his eyes again. "I can say with certainty, I haven't been to church since I got your Dear John letter. How about you? Be honest, it was your wedding day, right?"

"Right," Sarah murmured. "And that too was my mistake, he just wanted to run away and get married. He had been baptized Catholic, but he or his family didn't attend Mass or care to, but I insisted on a Catholic marriage. Had I not, we would be free to marry in church." She let out a disgruntled throaty grumble. "That was the one and only time he listened to me and now even that act is coming back to haunt me, isn't it?"

Tim opened his blue eyes and fixed his gaze at nothing. He ignored her question. "Please Sarah," he pleaded in a soft controlled voice. "I've never once asked you about your marriage. Not for a tiny detail. I don't want to know what your wedding dress looked like, how your hair was fixed, what the weather was like, who made what decisions, nothing, zero, zip!" His heart was beating fast. "I just want to hear what I cannot hear, that it never took place." He turned on his side away from Sarah. He didn't want her to see that his eyes were watering up.

Sarah reached out and touched his head and hair. "I just thought that is what you would want. To marry me in church."

Tim rolled himself up and sat on the edge of the bed with his back to her. "Christ, Sarah, of course that is what I wish to do, but it's only a wish!" He pushed both of his hands hard through his sandy hair. His mind was steaming to a boil now and he wanted to shout at her about his biggest pain. That he wanted her virginity and to give up his own to only her from the first time they kissed back at River's Bend High. But he didn't scream that wish to Sarah, or tell her that the odds of a young virile sailor remaining chaste while being exposed to the temptations of the Orient were in the trillions, but he had done that for her. Nor did he tell her at the first port of call his ship made after he received her sorrowful letter he practically flew to a Hong Kong whorehouse before the anchor settled on the sandy sea bottom. There he surrendered to a nameless indifferent stranger what he struggled to keep for her alone to claim.

He had the puritanical code of a boy scout then, but no knowledge on how to build a fire until he got burnt. He must've been out with the stars eating a Milky Way to have expected a lonesome beauty never to be tempted by the Adonis' her good looks would attract. Yet, he had avoided seduction by the beautiful for her sake. Was her love for him back then not as overwhelming as his love for her? Apparently it wasn't. What about now?

Sarah could feel his controlled wrath, but persisted on talking about what she felt had to be discussed. "Maybe I could get an annulment of my marriage. I was young, in a foolish state of mind, and now I know that he never intended to keep his vow to God, yet alone me…"

Sarah continued talking but Tim quit listening to her. His jealous thoughts were taking control of his mind, breaking through the foggy barrier of Sarah's love with ease. Painful memories were being called forth in anger, wanted and desired by their owner to strike at the heart of the one that causes his pain. He wanted to shout at her. "More like a foolish state of being horny!" But he clenched his teeth and swallowed the words. Sarah was still talking.

"I think he committed adultery many times. Maybe I could get an annulment?"

Tim jumped to his feet and paced the floor. "What do you think we did?" he said, pointing to her and then to himself. "Before your divorce was final, we committed adultery even in the civic sense. And as far as the church is concerned we are still breaking that commandment."

Sarah snapped her head back and stared at him. She had never seen him lose control of himself.

"Anyhow." He stopped his pacing, looked at her, and lowered his voice. "Annulments are a bunch of crap. Easy annulments and quick divorces cheapen marriage to the point that it's no longer deserving to be called a sacrament." He started pacing again. "The Church is making the same mistake as Moses, granting concessions out of pity to hard headed believers without scriptural authority. An annulment would only make us hypocrites, pretending something that happened never happened." He stopped again and looked at her. "What would an annulment make Lynn? A bastard?"

Sarah lowered her eyes. "I was just suggesting it as a way to make you happy." She started to cry and brought her knees up to her breasts and buried her face in her hands. Soon her tears turned to sobs and her body began to shake. She shook her head hard and shuddered, loosening her bunched up hair. It fell around her hands and face. The glimmering rays of the falling sun reflected off her trembling body.

Seeing her agonize in the darkening room, his anger with her retreated back into the limbo region of his mind. He crawled back onto the bed to her side and pulled her hands from her face. Her hair was in disarray, some wavy strands matted to her wet face. She looked at him with fiery eyes and raised her voice. "My mistakes have not been easy on me either!"

He tried to pull her against his chest but she would have none of his pity and pulled her hands from his, twisted away from his outreached hands, and got off the bed. She slowly slid down a corner of the room and onto the carpeted floor. The corner was darker than the rest of the room. Tim could see her huddled there, hunched over, hands around her knees, exposing her legs to faint gleams of amber sunlight. He sat on the rumpled bed watching her. He could hear her breathing. In contrition for what was happening between them, he fell sideways onto the sheets that still smelled of Sarah. He heard her sigh and talk softly to him.

"You're not fooling me, Tim. You hate me sometimes. Hate me for leaving you. Hate me for being foolish." She paused. "Stupid, really. But Tim, I have never claimed to be smart, not that you have, but you are, and everyone knows that." She sniffled. "In high school when you asked me to go steady with you I jumped with joy. How you hugged and kissed my youth away, eliminating all of the craziness for me that most girls suffer through in high school. I never had to worry about being popular. I was Tim Brogan's girl. The smartest guy in school loved me, and only me. Forget about football players or being a cheerleader, I needed none of it to be accepted by the crowd. I had the song and dance man in my corner and high school was a breeze. Life was a breeze for me until you left my side and went into the Navy." She sniffled and gave off a deep sigh and rubbed her eyes. She was sobbed out and collecting her thoughts.

Tim just lay there like a cadaver staring at her outlined figure as the last glimmering rays of sunshine faded from the room. In the darkness, Sarah began speaking to him again in a calm voice. "Tim, those trips we took to Pittsburgh, the plays, the musicals, art shows, and our conversations. Just being with you when you speak with other people makes me feel very special to be holding onto your arm."

Tim couldn't see her squeezing her hands together. Sarah was trying to settle herself down, calm her troubling mind while making her own struggles with her past clear to him.

When Sarah's form completely disappeared into the dark corner, Tim rolled onto his back and put his hands behind his head. He knew Sarah was picking and choosing each word that she spoke to him. Again she began softly with his name.

"Tim, our families are very ethnic, you know that. But you're an only child, and you don't belong to a large family, a clan I suppose, like I do. My family doesn't understand divorce anymore than your family. But I have so many more people to contend with, I get such pity thrown at me. Divorce is a selfish act to them. They only understand work, sacrifice, worship, and commitment to marriage. Nothing to them should break up a marriage. There is no divorce in my family. It's foreign and shameful and sinful to allow selfishness to run your life. Woe to that person on judgment day. God, you should hear the names they call him for leaving me."

Tim could hear her shifting in the corner, and hoped she would come back into their bed without calling out to her to do so. He didn't know what to say to her so he kept hoping that soon she would come into his arms. But she didn't and he spoke to her. "Come back to bed, Sarah."

"Not yet, Tim, I have more to say to you, and please listen without any acid comments."

"Go on, I'll keep quiet."

"I was raised to be no more than a figurine doll on a shelf. to be looked at and desired by young men as they went about the business of the world making money. No one, not even you, encouraged me to be self-reliant or independent. Looking back on the girls I went to high school with, I think Bonnie was the smart one. She always had confidence in herself on stage with you and in her studies. Other girls laughed at her behind her back, because of her thinness. They called her names like bones, and the boys took advantage of her loneliness and made fun of her too."

Sarah stood, Tim could hear her and his heart jumped thinking that she was coming to him. But she didn't and she paced the room in the darkness releasing her long held thoughts to the man she loved. Tim had not had a cigarette for a long time, but he now had the strong urge to puff. Sarah continued.

"Tim, sometimes I think Bonnie wasn't the fool our friends all made her out to be. She learned to be independent. Her looks weren't taking her anywhere, so she compensated by using her brains. She has a nice and interesting job now as a legal aid, while many of the girls that made fun of her are quickly becoming second hand dolls with babies to care for and no skills to face the world. I can't believe it's 1962 and how fast I screwed up my life. But you have given me a second chance at happiness, and I want to protect that chance." She stopped walking somewhere in the dark room.

Tim could hear her tightening her robe around her nakedness, tying the cloth cord taut against her waist. She spoke to him in a raised and sharp voice.

"Tim, you have to accept that I was married. That I made love to someone other than you. We can't have a life together by blocking out what happened. It will be with us for the rest of our lives. One day Lynn is going to want to know about her Dad, so there is no running away from my former marriage. Just continuing to live together is not going to change the past, but I'm willing to do that for you if that is what you want. But, Tim, I want so much to be your wife." She started to cry again.

Tim rose up on the bed to move to her, but she heard the sound of his moving body and stopped him. "Wait Tim, please." She sobbed.

Tim fell back down and held a pillow to his heart.

"Tim, I don't want to watch you brood anymore about me and my failed marriage. I know our relationship is different than what other divorced women face. Few women return to their high school sweetheart after divorce. Usually that is who they got divorced from, so I know it's different between us. I crushed your feelings by not waiting for you and now I'm asking you to close that wound I caused as if nothing had ever happened between us. That's a big request, I know, and I don't know if it can be done if you don't lighten up."

No sound came from off the bed, not even a sigh; Sarah couldn't even hear him breathing. "Are you okay, Tim?" she whispered.

"I'm all right." Tim whispered back to her. He heard her fumbling with the stereo. Peggy Lee's voice came to him in the darkness and so did Sarah. They groped for each other.

CHAPTER SIX

After Sarah's talk with him in their bedroom, Tim became more honest with her. When Mr. Murky came with his reel of torment, he would tell Sarah he was slipping into depression and if loving him wasn't enough, she'd come up with other distracting ideas. Sometimes they would go to his parents' house just so he could play piano. That always cheered him up and little Lynn loved the merry tunes he could play for her. Often Sarah was tired after work, but when he needed his piano, she pushed for them to go to his childhood home. She knew at times the upright was a better cure for his healing heart than her hugs. He was beating Mr. Murky and healing his crushed heart.

It was Halloween evening and Tim had brought Lynn back inside their own apartment after trick and treating the apartment building neighbors and a few nearby houses. Tim spread all of her collection of goodies onto the kitchen table where he, with Lynn on his lap, inspected the sugary treasure before allowing the little girl to feast on the sweets. She had dressed up like a honeybee, a costume her grandmother had made for her. Except for the wings, which still protruded from her back, the rest of the costume now lay scattered about the kitchen floor.

When Lynn did start eating, she only took small nibbles from a piece of candy before her little hands dropped it and reached out for a different kind to unwrap and taste. Sarah had warned him not to let Lynn eat too much candy before she left for work. Brogan finished off her discarded pieces by eating the evidence.

Tim was gathering up the candy into her collection bag, and telling her that they must save the rest of the candy to show Mommy, when the loud knock on the door came and sounded so disturbing that it frightened the little girl and startled Tim.

After opening the door, Brogan quickly lost all misgivings about answering the door to such a threatening sound. Standing before him with a wide grin and in his green Marine uniform was John, Sergeant stripes neatly sewn to his big arms and wearing several rows of ribbons.

"Jesus, John!" Tim burst into laughter. "You scared the hell out of me! You knock on the door like a bill collector!"

John just reached out and pulled Tim into his chest and mumbled. "It's good to be home," which surprised Tim after having had witnessed John's happiness in Japan. Tim struggled out of John's ape grip, looked his buddy over, and was startled for the second time. The Marine had watery eyes.

"John, what is this all about?" Brogan asked pointing to the purple ribbon. "Isn't that a purple heart?"

"Yeah, but don't make me a hero, I was just at the wrong place at the wrong time."

Tim's mouth was half open. He mumbled. "But we're not at war."

"Mind if I sit?" John asked and took up a chair at the table beside Lynn. "And who is this little butterfly?"

Tim chuckled. "Honeybee, John," and pointed out the rest of the bee parts on the floor.

John threw his hands into the air. "And what a honey she is!"

"Well, what about those ribbons?" Tim asked slamming the door closed.

"We're at war, Tim; the American people just don't know it yet. It's called Vietnam. Hey, you got some coffee? I was out last night, the Social Club with Cousin Orson, Fitch, Dutch, and a few others." John chuckled. "That damn Dutch is as cheap as ever, we had to all ride his ass to spring for a round."

"Sure, sure," Tim uttered, "I could go for a cup myself. We have a lot of catching up to do. But let me tell you, I'm so happy to see you." Tim went about the small kitchen preparing to serve his guest while John took up with Lynn, teasing her. "I think I'll eat all that candy." He started rubbing his belly. "Hmmmm, I like candy."

Lynn stared at him wide-eyed.

"Who's candy is that?" he asked her.

Lynn didn't answer him.

"Is that yours?"

She nodded her head.

"What's your name?"

She murmured, "Lynn."

"Can I eat all this candy?" John asked reaching over the table and gathering it into a big pile in front of him. "I have a big belly to put it in."

Lynn turned to Tim for help.

"He's just kidding you, Lynn. Smack his hand and he'll leave the candy alone." And she did. John acted like he'd been shot and slowly rolled off the chair onto the floor. Lynn started laughing and before Tim served up the coffee, Lynn was being tossed about and played with like she'd never been played with before. She was screaming with joy and her gladness did not go unnoticed by Brogan.

He had always been attentive to Lynn, played games with her, read to her, played the piano for her, and he loved her. But he never got the response that John was now getting. Her eyes sparkled like diamonds while crawling all over John's big frame lying on his back on the tile floor.

"Perhaps all that time wasted in the past brooding over Sarah and Mr. Murky should have been spent tossing Lynn into the air." he thought while pouring coffee into John's cup. "Coffee's up!" He bellowed over Lynn's screams and giggles to John on the floor.

It took some time for Lynn to settle down after they got off of the floor. John held her on his lap. She just didn't want to quit playing with her newfound big stuffed gorilla friend. Tim noticed that John's movements off the floor and getting himself back into the kitchen chair were slow and careful.

"Where were you hit, John? And tell me everything. I'm going crazy here. I thought you were still in Japan. I was expecting to see you showing up in Rivers Bend with Kimiko someday."

John tossed his head back. "In the ass, in my big ass is where I got hit. And Kimiko, who knows where she's at. But wherever it is, I'm sure she's making lots of yen." He swallowed a half of a cup of black coffee. Tim slid the glass pot across the tabletop so that the Marine could help himself, which he did, and sighed. "Where to begin, so much has happened since we were together in Japan."

"From that point on," Tim smiled, "would be good."

"Well, I re-enlisted of course, for three years, and everything was just fine, except that Kimiko wouldn't change her mind about marrying me. She was goin' to live and die in Japan, end of story. That was the summer of 1960, right after your visit. But what I didn't know at the time, was that American military advisors were being sent to Southeast Asia, Vietnam, Thailand, two places I know of, to train their military forces, and in Vietnam a little bit more than training. American advisors were and still are going on missions with the South Vietnam regulars and running airdrops. About a year after I re-enlisted, my unit was ordered out of Japan, to Okinawa. And a battalion at a time was embarked aboard ship to cruise the China Sea as a ready landing force in case anything went wrong and some Americans needed rescuing." He paused.

Lynn had fallen sound asleep. Tim took the little girl from John and put her into her bed, then got back to John anxious to hear the remainder of his story. He poured more coffee for both of them and brewed another pot while John continued.

"My battalion didn't sail at first, so I'm just sittin' on Okinawa missing Kimiko and my pad, wasting away the two years the Corps had agreed to let me stay stationed in Japan for giving them a three year hitch. After six months on Okinawa, I go aboard ship with my battalion. We're out a month or so floating around on a helicopter carrier when we get orders to rescue an American aircrew. While dropping supplies to a South Vietnam force in a fire fight, the aircraft crashed, but not in South Vietnam, but north in the DMZ. A no man's land that separates the two countries, north and south." John swallowed the rest of his coffee. Tim got the fresh pot from the coffee maker and refilled both cups.

"Before that time, my squad couldn't have shown you Vietnam on a map. We were told it's gonna be rapid. Drop in—get the hell out mission. No engagement with any hostiles expected. Some of the crew is alive, getting SOS's from the jungle, half a mile inside the DMZ. The plan was to drop a platoon and some corpsmen onto the crash site; take up defensive positions while the aircrew is cared for and lifted out. Then the platoon would march south while the rest of the battalion at a LZ across the border moved north through the jungle in support of the platoon withdraw." John chuckled. "In and out."

"Your platoon went in?" Tim asked.

"Naw, I trooped north. There wasn't a goddamned shot fired. The air crew was rescued, the Battalion joined up as planned, crossed back over into South Vietnam. That's all I remember. Someone behind me stepped on a mine and I had half my ass blown off. I woke up in a Field Hospital. Then I was sent to Saigon, then to Hawaii, then to San Diego. Some General came to my sick bay in Saigon, pinned some medals on me, and thanked me for a job well done and for leaving half my ass in the jungle."

"And Kimiko?" Tim asked.

"Photos and memories. I tried to contact her, got a hold of Mama-san by phone from Hawaii. She said Kimiko go home. Osaka." John chuckled. "Probably went home to count her damn yen."

"Are you out now?"

"I'll be medically discharged by Christmas. I flew home on emergency leave."

"Emergency?" Tim looked puzzled.

"Yeah, my mother died."

Tim felt bad. He'd been so squirreled away with Sarah avoiding all of their friends that he had not gotten the news. "I'm sorry, John."

John waved off his condolences without comment.

"What funeral home is..."

John cut him off. "No services. I held my own service. She's already ashes."

"What did you say?" Tim asked thinking he didn't hear what he thought he heard.

"You heard me right, Brogan. I got into town, went right to Reilly's funeral home. Told him to burn her and do whatever he wanted with her ashes. And amen, that was the end of the service!"

Tim didn't know what to say, so he didn't say anything, just drank coffee while John went on to another subject.

"I have a lot of money saved up. Tomorrow I'm meeting with a realtor and flop down a big payment on a garage down by the bridge. The guy that owns it now is retiring, goin' to Florida. A nice place, I'm getting his garage and all his equipment. I'm not working for anyone when I get out, but myself." He chuckled. "Who's goin' hire a half ass mechanic anyhow? I should be able to make it okay, and besides, I'll be getting a nice disability check from the Veterans Administration. At least that's what they tell me."

"You must've got it bad?"

John grimaced. "Let's just say I don't have beach buns. Then he burst into laughter. "But then again, I never did!"

Tim laughed with him and admired his ability to toss aside his problems. The exception being the wound his mother gave him.

John slapped down on the table. "Well, I told those guys at the club that I'd drag your wholesome ass out tonight for a few beers, but I can see this baby sittin' thing keeps you tied down. They told me you and Sarah just about hibernate."

Tim smiled. "Just about."

"I met Gypsy last night. What a trip! I like her. Too bad Orson's screwing her and getting over on Fitch. She didn't tell me of course, Orson did. Just gotta brag about himself. My cousin can be such a pig sometimes, messin' over his friends." John winked at Tim. "Then again who are we to condemn, but it is different when the woman is a wife and mother."

Kimiko jumped right into Tim's guilty mind and suddenly the coffee tasted sickly. His stomach did a flip-flop. Did John just send him a signal that he knew about his romp with Kimiko?

Tim stammered for something to say. "Ah, yeah, in a way, I guess, ahh, committing adultery is bad stuff. And mightily hard to be repentant for, and I guess hard to be forgiven for." He felt perplexed and quit talking.

"How's Sarah doin'?" John smiled and changed the subject. "I was glad to hear the two of you got back together."

"Fine." Tim uttered.

"That guy she married must've been a real jerk." John stated. "Orson was telling me he came to the club one night acting like an ass at the bar, telling everyone how much money he made, wearing a goofy looking tie and…"

John's words hit Tim's ears so hard everything else John was saying to him were words wasted on a dead man. Orson's words came rushing back to him like a comet from afar. Orson had said that he had seen Sarah's husband at the Club one time. If Orson was at the club on the same night as her husband it had to be after Orson was discharged from the Navy, and Sarah was living on her own. Orson had said that the very day he arrived home after being discharged; he helped Sarah move into this apartment. Not from her home in East Pittsburgh, but from her parents' house where she first lived after being abandoned. Orson said Sarah and her husband left the club arm in arm on the night he saw them there, with him giving Orson a victory salute as a good-bye gesture. The night they left the club arm in arm they were living apart, so where did they go that night? Mr. Murky was here! In this apartment! In their bedroom! In their bed? John was still talking about Orson.

"And I'm telling you Brogan, as my good friend; don't ever let that bastard alone near Sarah. He got this urge…"

Tim always felt Orson had a desire for Sarah in high school, but Orson had a desire for all shapely women back then and ran from one girl to the next dragging his desires behind him. What John was saying now, however, was shocking and new to him and put all thoughts about Mr. Murky on hold.

"…she was all alone. If I know Orson he pushed himself hard on her, taking full advantage…"

Tim put his hand to his forehead. "What is John saying?" he thought. "That Orson and Sarah made love? Naw, he's not saying that, is he?"

"…I like Sarah and you; I'm only bringing this up because last night he told me point blank he wanted a stab at her again…"

Tim leaned back in his chair. This can't be happening.

"…but he said that you keep her tucked away and he can't…"

"John, I'm getting sick!" Tim rushed from the table, his mind whirling with rampaging thoughts.

Did Orson know his best-kept secret as well as he knew Fitch's best kept secret? And was Mr. Murky in their apartment, in their bedroom, on the bed with Sarah?

Murky was jumping up and down in his head, laughing, and dancing, doing flips, twirling his fat yellow neon tie. Up and down, up and down, up and down...Tim threw his head into the toilet bowl and the candy and coffee sprayed from his mouth. He heaved again and again until his stomach ached and emptied. Brogan was lightheaded and only wanted to go and lay in bed. John walked him to the bed and then telephoned Sarah at work.

He could hear John talking to Sarah on the telephone. He heard him hang up the receiver. He heard him cleaning up the bathroom mess. He heard Sarah rush into the apartment and speak to John. He heard Sarah open the bedroom door and softly call out his name, but he didn't answer her and pretended he was asleep. He heard Sarah going into Lynn's room to check on her. He heard Sarah leaving Lynn's bedroom. He heard Sarah making coffee. He heard Sarah and John talking about his sudden sickness. He heard them talking about old times. He heard Sarah come into the bedroom to check on him again, but he didn't open his eyes. He heard John say good-bye to Sarah and that he'd see her at Christmastime. He heard Sarah taking a shower. He heard Sarah climbing into bed. He felt Sarah beside himself. She put her arm around him.

CHAPTER SEVEN

Tim missed an entire week of work. Sarah kept plugging along at her job. She was doing her very best to understand his illness and nurse him back to good health, but by now she was beginning to suspect his sickness was more mental than physical and much more to do about her past then he was letting on.

She poured the tea Tim had asked for soon after she got home from work. She did not have any tea in the apartment so she walked to the convenience store nearby and purchased a large box of Kleenex along with the tea. She had the feeling that her relationship with Tim was about to end and this time forever.

The walk in the cold air did her some good, awakening her from the moping feeling she acquired since Tim's latest bout of depression. But by the time she returned to the apartment, she was shivering with only an angora sweater and slacks on to keep her warm.

She carried the cup of steaming hot tea to Tim's bedside table along with the box of tissue and sat down next to him on the bed.

"Do you feel strong enough to talk, Tim?"

He smiled at her and took her hand into his. "It's time, Amante."

"What happened, Tim? What happened when John was here?"

Tim propped himself up against the headboard and sipped some tea. A few drops fell onto his pajamas. He smiled at her. "Mr. Murky almost killed me this time. John said a few unintentional words that set off a reaction in my mind. A sort of jealous explosion. I've been laying here on my back thinking for a week. I'm twenty six years old and have nothing in common with any of my old friends. Nothing. It wouldn't hurt me a bit if I never saw any of them again. That's not normal behavior for a young man. I think I've obtained somewhere along in my life grave mental problems, a disease, and I think it's getting worse. And I believe, Sarah," he paused and took her hand. "I believe it started aboard ship after I received your Dear John letter. I know for certain from that moment on I have never been the same and I began to act so far out of character that on occasion I couldn't stomach myself. I don't know if I should just take my things and go when I get a little better, or is it worth talking about?"

Sarah squeezed his hand. "Anything is worth a try, Tim. You're worthwhile to me. Tim, you were always different than the rest of us growing up. Sometimes brilliantly funny, and at other times, far away in thought. We had so much fun in high school, me and you, and the rest of our group, and a lot of that was because of your talents and energy to make learning fun."

"But back then," he paused and sipped his tea. "I wanted to be out and about having fun with the gang. Now I just want to live in a cocoon." He smiled. "And keep you wrapped up with me."

Sarah reached over and lifted his chin. They gazed at each other. Tim spoke. "You're a stunning woman, Sarah. Sometimes, like now, with that burnt orange sweater on, your dark hair and glistening green eyes, you overwhelm me with desire," he chuckled softly. "Lust really. I never had such lust for another woman. I made love to other women, but only after you left me."

Sarah turned her eyes away but squeezed his hand hard. Tim continued.

"After I got your letter of good-bye, I abandoned myself to one whore after another. From port to port I paid for sexual intercourse. I was trying to use sex to drive you out of my mind or pretend that the whores were you, I don't know which. I was always drunk. Maybe I wanted to believe in that old broken heart remedy you hear people quote about broken relationships. That there's a lot of fish in the ocean, but there really wasn't any other fish for me in any ocean... or anywhere else that they may swim."

Sarah was crying. "Do you want me to stop?" he asked.

"No, no please, Tim. This is what we need to do, if we will have any chance at all. I understand more now. You love me more than it's possible for me to grasp. I more than hurt you. I crucified you."

"Other shipmates told me I'd get over you. Dear John's come to a lot of sailors and most I suppose do get over it. But not me. At sea, between port calls, it was like my own garden of Gethsemane. I was crying out to God in my prayers like Jesus did, begging him to let this bitter cup handed to me pass me by. But unlike Jesus, I couldn't utter the words, 'but thy will be done'. Because if that was God's will, that I lose you, then God didn't care if I lost my very soul."

Sarah sighed loud. Brogan continued. "Everyday when the helicopter came to the ship for a mail drop, my heart filled with hope that there would be a letter from you, but there never was an envelope of hope mailed to me. It was only me and Jesus and God's big ocean to ride out the storm raging in my heart and mind.

Sarah reached over and turned the bedside lamp off and fell into Tim's lap. He stroked her hair and continued speaking to her. "When I had a port call, I burnt myself out on top of whores like a lot of other young sailors do, but they were having fun. I wanted to be like them, but it didn't work out that way for me. How many times I stood at the rail, looking back at the wake from our ship, wanting to be a part of the wake, to be washed away in a moment of turbulence and then maybe the fright boiling inside of me would pass to a dead calm. Then I could ask God. Why? Why did I lose you? Why didn't he show me any mercy? Why do the good suffer? And I thought I was good. I tried to live by his rules. One of the passages in the Bible always made perfect sense to me. It's where Jesus says mankind wasn't made for the law, but that the law was made for mankind. Everyone else seemed to think that the commandments are just a lot of 'Thou shall nots,' party pooping rules to make our lives unhappy and restrictive. But I knew what Jesus was speaking of. He was giving us a blueprint for a happy life, the commandments are a blueprint to build a life upon, not a form of slavery with stern rules and punishment. Violating them brings down upon us our own punishment. The only tools needed to utilize God's blueprints are to have the desire to put aside selfishness and the willingness to treat your fellow beings with honor. Only those blinded by selfish stubbornness think they can live without God. Even the pagans cry out for a God, and if they don't find one, they make themselves up an idol." Tim kept gently stroking her hair. "Am I going overboard with my thoughts?"

Sarah reached into her own hair and took his hand. "No Tim, you are your thoughts."

"What John said last week jarred my mind back to the night we got back together at the club, something that Orson had said to me about you. I suddenly realized that there was more to your separation than I was led to believe. It wasn't complete abandonment." Tim was frank. "You slept with Mr. Murky in this apartment?"

Sarah sighed.

Tim didn't show any response to her heavy sigh. He already knew the answer. He spoke to her in a gentle voice. "Sarah, it's not you, it's me. You had every right to sleep with your husband even if you were separated. I think I know what occurred. He came to Rivers Bend with a change of heart, probably promising you to be a better husband and father and you gave him a chance, but for some reason or another it just didn't work out. Am I about right?"

He could hear Sarah wiping her eyes. He kept running his hand through her hair.

"Hold me tight, Tim."

He did.

"Tim, I lied to you... my husband didn't leave me. I left him." She waited for a response. None came.

"I couldn't stand being around him. I couldn't stand making love to him. I couldn't stand his bragging. I couldn't stand being dressed up and taken to company parties like a salesman of the year award and being shown off to his fellow hustlers as a prize. Watching him being patted on the back for snagging me, a real beauty you know their type praises... being heaped on him because he married me. He just made me sick. Everything was money, everything was a show. And kiss ass, there was none better at that than my husband. He would even let the regional bosses flirt with me just to advance his standing. What an ass he was, Tim." She sniffled.

"Hold me tighter, Tim." she pleaded. "One day, I'm not even certain which day it was, I got Lynn and left while he was out showing off somewhere. I came back home and lied to my parents. Told them he was cheating on me." she sighed. "They would never understand me walking out just because my husband is a jackass."

"Did he run around on you?"

"I don't know. He was gone a lot. There were always sweet odors on his clothes. He wore so many lotions himself, he made me gag. He could have cheated on me, but I don't know if he really did or not. I didn't care if he did. It was him; I couldn't stand to look at him. And it was you. I knew you would be coming home soon. I had hidden hope that you would take me back just as if nothing ever happened...almost worked out the way I hoped."

Tim questioned her softly. "If you couldn't stand him, why did you end up sleeping here with him? I don't understand."

"He started calling me up. Crying and begging me to come back to him. Telling me to think about Lynn and the good future I was taking away from her. He did do well. Lynn or I never wanted for anything. So he came to the Social Club. I wasn't expecting him. He just came on his own and waited at the bar until I finished bowling. By the time I joined him at the bar, he had half the steel workers throwing up in their beers, that's how bad he was putting on his act. I was embarrassed for me, for him, and my lovely daughter. We went off into a quiet corner and talked things out, but I refused to go back with him and told him I was filing for divorce. He gave up trying to change my mind and accepted the reality of our parted lives. He then asked if he could see Lynn before leaving Rivers Bend and I agreed. We left the club." Tim interrupted her.

"Arm in arm?"

"Hell no, who told you that?"

"Orson."

"Figures." she murmured. "That's another story." She took his hand to her lips and kissed it softly. "I didn't have a car at the time and it was about ten o'clock, so we rode together to get Lynn at my parent's house. I hated waking her up. Normally on Friday nights after bowling and the dance, I'd just pick her up in the morning, but I went and got her for his sake, and we brought her back here. She slept through the whole ordeal and I put her to bed. Then he asked to sleep over so that he could see Lynn in the morning. I told him he had to sleep on the sofa. I made a pot of coffee, thinking he'd want to talk about the terms of our separation, visitation for Lynn, things like that, but all he wanted to do was make love. He started begging to do it one last time, it was deplorable. I couldn't shut him up. That's when I decided to take him up on his offer. He said if I let him have his way, afterwards he'd leave and never bother me or Lynn again. By then I didn't even want him to be Lynn's father or care if he supported her, I just yearned for the sight of him to evaporate. I took a chance that what he was saying would come to pass. And it did. We've never heard from him since."

Tim questioned. "How did you ever fall for him in the first place? That's what is really hard for me to accept, that you actually fell for him enough to marry him."

"I turn that over in my mind almost constantly, Tim. I was working at the restaurant and he came in one day with such a friendly attitude, talking to everyone and being real nice and polite. So week after week he came, took a fancy to me and started asking the other girls about me. They were all urging me to go out with him, and to put some fun into my life. I was awfully bored. On my nineteenth birthday, the other girls at the restaurant had a little party for me after we closed up. Nothing big, just some cake and coffee and funny gifts. To my surprise, he shows up with flowers and candy, and believe this or not, a violinist. It was a fast little party and he asked to drive me home, and everyone was urging me to go with him, so I did. And it started that way, slow, and I guess I was drawn in by the attention I was getting from him, and the girls at work who seemed both excited and envious. I was still writing you love letters and going out with him. I felt terrible about that, but I wasn't sure about anything and I was wishing you were home so I could make up my mind." She kissed his hand hard.

"That is when I asked Bonnie what I should do. She told me to write to you. He was eight years older than me, had money, independent, and seemed to me to know everything about life. He asked me to quit working so we could be together every night. I did and he gave me spending money and started coming to my house every night and we'd sit around. He'd bring my parents gifts and before I knew it, I felt like I belonged to him. I became dependent on him just like my mother and aunts are dependent on their husbands. It's just so hard to explain when you don't know yourself why you did such a dumb thing."

"You're doing fine." Tim whispered.

"Did you ever make a new friend when you were about nine or ten years old? It was like that. You meet this new friend and she's new and different, and you're so happy about your new friend that you shun your old faithful friends just to be with the new friend. The new friend is special. She has new ideas, does different things, and you're taken in by the new friend. You don't realize that the new friend is controlling you, keeping you away from your old friends by making sly comments, or making plans for the both of you that will avoid meeting up with the old friends. And then slowly you start to see through your new friend, and if you're lucky you can run back to your old friends if they're not too offended with you. That's how it was with me and my husband. That's the best I can explain it, Tim. I got some of my old friends back, but do I have you?"

Tim didn't answer her question but asked his own. "What's this about Orson?"

She held his hand against her lips and spoke through his fingers. "He hates me. On the day I moved into this apartment, a bunch of the gang helped me, including Orson. Well, afterwards, I bought some beer and lunchmeat and we enjoyed ourselves. I felt so good being back home, in my own apartment, with my old friends. I felt just like I was back in high school. We kidded each other, talked about you and everybody else that hung out with us. I felt great. We had music playing, we roughed house each other, the girls would sit on the guys laps, it was all in fun, nothing was planned, things were just happening…"

Orson's words again came back to Tim. Was Sarah meowing? Meowing, "it just happened." Meowing, "it wasn't planned." Maybe Orson is the one that is right about women and not God. Be selfish, the women understand selfish men and meow to be nudged along and seduced by ally cats.

"…late, so I needed someone to drive me over to my mother's house to get Lynn. Orson volunteered. Everyone else went home. It was dark outside. I was still in a very cheery mood. Orson pulled off onto River Road and I was stunned. He parked the car and made some forceful moves on me. I was afraid and shocked into silence. He pushed me against the door and held me tight. I knew he had intentions of forcibly raping me if I resisted him. I could see the intense lust in his eyes." She paused. "When he kissed me, I kissed him back. He was overheated, had his hands all over me. I whispered to him in my best seductive voice; 'Why here Orson, when I have a bed at the apartment?' He didn't stop right away, I had to quit kissing back and tell him I wasn't a schoolgirl, and I wasn't doing it in the car. I acted excited, but I was in a panic. His grip was hurting me. Finally he listened and I made him drive to my mother's house to get Lynn, promising him that she'd be fast asleep and no bother to his plans for the two of us." She kissed Tim's palm.

"He drove fast, even ran a red light. He pulled up in front of my parent's house; I said I'd be only a minute. I ran into the house and slammed the door shut and stayed all night. He waited outside with the engine running and headlights on for over twenty minutes. I watched him through the window. When it dawned on him that I wasn't coming out to play, he laid tire rubber down the road. Ever since that time he hates me and will say rude things to me when no one else is around."

"Like what?"

"Do you really want to know? It may hurt your feelings."

"I want to know."

"The last time I saw Orson alone was the night we got back together. I ran into him in the rest room passageway at the club. He said 'Tim's waiting for you in the dance hall, but he's not wearing a big ugly tie, so you won't be serving it up to him tonight, either!'"

"So Orson was trying to get over on me?" Tim uttered.

Sarah sat up on the bed. "Tim, did you hear what you just said?"

"What do you mean?"

"Orson wasn't trying to get over on you. When he made his pass at me we had no relationship whatsoever. We only had a past that neither one of us was obligated to. You see Tim, that's our problem, you know the facts but in your mind they don't matter."

Tim switched the lamp on and drank his cold tea in one gulp. "I do know the facts, Sarah, and they shouldn't matter, but they do. My heart is welded to you and it's weighted down by our past. I don't know if I'll ever recover from that hollow feeling that penetrated my body at the ship's railing after reading your letter. My happy life stopped there and I went from whores to books to you to find some peace of mind, but it never came to me and still hasn't. I'm sure it never will. I was watching John last week playing with Lynn. I never saw her so happy. If I'm here living with you throwing my fits of gloom it can only..."

Sarah's face turned pale. She realized what was happening. It was over. She sobbed. "Tim, please. Please stay!"

"Sarah I must go and live apart from you. It's better for all of us, especially Lynn. Who knows how deep my depression will sink? I feel now that it's a lifetime depression I've contacted and there are no magic pills to make it disappear. It could end up making us hate one another. How terrible that would be. I'd rather be dead. Lynn doesn't need a zombie walking around in her life, she needs a Dad."

Sarah was sobbing loud. Tim held her all night long and in the morning he left her still lying on the bed.

CHAPTER EIGHT

Separation from Sarah was endured by Tim. Christmastime came without cheer and he couldn't wait for the holiday spirit to pass on so that he didn't have to pretend he was happy or say the word merry in any form. His life consisted of going to work and then going home to his childhood bedroom. Only there in the solitude of his bedroom did he feel free from a pestering world. Sarah never called or tried to contact him and he resisted the urges that came over him to rush to her side. With steel determination to avoid her at all cost and believing that they all would be the worst for it if they got back together, he checked off his pains one day at a time...one ache at a time.

Little Lynn and Sarah deserved a better life than he would be able to provide. He felt close to losing his job at the paint factory. Comments had been made about his forgetfulness and tardiness, and that is the main reason he had not sought a place of his own to live. Soon he believed he might once again be completely dependent upon his parents. That thought did not please him but he felt unable to do anything about it. Sometimes he wished he was still in the Navy where life is so regimented it would be a blessing to be forced to go from one daily function to another. He would have to get a menial job, something without much thought and the boss would be most happy just to see him show up for work.

The bridge out of town was icy. The paint factory was ten miles away. He would be late for work again. His car crossed over the river and Tim drove off the suspension bridge. Several automobiles were haphazardly parked off to the side of the road, abandoned by their owners in the late December snow storm. The all night storm was over but the road crews were not able to keep up with the demand to clear the main roads after such a heavy snow. Traffic was backed up. Tim stepped on the gas pedal. His car made slippery fishtail movements up to the rear of the car in front of him.

Tim could see the Piano Bar; its blue and green neon sign glowing in the overcast morning. He had never been inside the bar. Red brake lights flashed on the car in front of him, traffic stopped.

The electric sign mounted on the roof of the Piano Bar blinked 'open...open...open' beckoning the drivers to come in out of the cold. Several cars were driving to the green concrete block building. A whim came over Tim. He turned towards the blinking lights and parked his car.

Inside the building the air was warm, smelling like pine deodorant. Holiday lights and decorations dangled throughout the tavern. Ben was behind the bar smiling at Tim. "Welcome, Piano Man."

Tim forced a smile, nodded, and was surprised that the bartender remembered him after only meeting him for a very brief encounter over two years ago at the Social Club.

The floor surrounding the horseshoe bar was cluttered with small tables, empty chairs, an elevated platform and the baby grand. Men stood around the bar, lunch buckets at hand, not mindful of Tim entering or Ben's salutation.

Ben stretched his left and normal arm across the bar. "Nice to see you."

Tim shook Ben's hand firmly. Ben smiled. "What's your poison?"

"Highball." Tim took a seat on the stool and suddenly had a craving for a cigarette. He went to the machine and bought a pack, came back to the bar and lit up. After the first couple puffs, it tasted good to him.

Ben brought two drinks on a tray. "Buy one, get one free, till noon during the week."

A customer played the jukebox. It was a love song. Tim, holding his highball to his lips, instantly knew the remedy to live with his undefeated pain. Here, not at the paint makers, or under blankets in his bed, but here, he could endure his life playing the piano. He drank both highballs quickly and ordered refills. Life could be tolerated here, moods penetrated with chemicals, sorrows enhanced to a melancholy acceptance. Ben came with his refills.

Ben wiped his hands on his apron, the white cloth tightly wrapped around his expanded belly. After inspecting his fingernails, he fiddled with his rose-colored bow tie. "I've asked the others about you. They say they never see you."

"Been staying to myself." Tim put his cigarette inside the ashtray, stood and took off his scarf and overcoat and tossed them over an empty stool.

Tim glanced at Ben's deformed arm and hand. Ben caught him looking. "My umbilical cord got tangled around it. I grew in the womb but this arm couldn't keep up with me. I can only lift it so high."

Brogan was lost for words and changed the subject. "You weren't sporting that mustache the last time. were you? Or was I that drunk?"

Ben laughed. "No, I keep it waxed. Nice, isn't it? It grows better than the red hair on my head."

The song on the jukebox ended. Tim took a deep drag on his cigarette. "Is that job still open, Ben? I quit my job five minutes ago."

Ben smiled. "More than ever." And pointed to the baby grand.

Tim followed Ben's arm to the piano, and, for a moment Sarah, was not on his mind. He walked to the baby grand, loosened his tie, unbuttoned his collar, opened and closed his hand exercise his long fingers. To play piano, make money, and drink for free, he wished for nothing more at this time in his life.

"Sing along stuff." Ben called out to him. "That's what the customers like."

CHAPTER NINE

Orson parked the car. He left the engine running and the heater on. The parking lot wasn't well lit and Orson deliberately parked in a darker spot then he had to. They chatted. Orson was speaking.

"Too bad the Marines couldn't discharge you before the holidays; you missed out on some good parties."

John didn't answer his cousin. He was starting to be a little apprehensive about Orson's true motives for coming to the Steak and Ale. Earlier that evening they had been to the Piano Bar. Tim had welcomed him back home with a few sing along songs that most of the customers joined them in singing. After several hours, Orson guided him to a few more bars around town to celebrate his homecoming. It had been a fun evening and the both of them were feeling the alcohol they'd gleefully consumed. When they had left the last drinking hole, John thought Orson was taking him to another bar in town. Rivers Bend, like most steel towns, had an abundance of taverns and Orson, who could be charming and funny in a crude sort of way, knew all of the bartenders by name.

"Aren't we goin' in for a drink?" John asked. "I could go for food, too."

"Too late to eat." Orson looked at his watch. "Almost midnight."

John gave a concerned look. "Okay cuz, what's up?"

Orson smiled without looking at John, gazing straight ahead through the windshield into the night and the well lit Steak and Ale building off in the distance. "Sarah."

"What about Sarah?" John quizzed opening his heavy winter jacket.

"Her car's not running. She needs a ride home and I'm offering my services." Orson pointed. "She'll be coming out of that kitchen door in about ten minutes."

"I take it this will all be a surprise to her?" John chuckled. "Orson, you have no chance with Sarah and you know it! Let's go."

"You don't know that. Circumstances change between people." Orson opened his jacket and pulled a cigarette out from his inside shirt pocket and lit it. He took a deep drag and blew the smoke at the windshield. "Anyhow, she still owes me an explanation for something that happened between us a long time ago."

John lit a cigarette too and took a few drags before he spoke. "And I'm here for support or some other naughty reason?"

Orson chuckled. "Yeah, don't be mad. She hasn't seen you since you came home. I'm using you to break the ice, have an excuse to talk to her. Okay?"

"Okay...but keep it on the level. I know you have a hard-on for her."

Orson howled. "Like you and the rest of the gang don't extend one for her!"

John shook his head. "Yeah, well maybe we do, but we're a lot more polite about it than you when it comes to our hankering."

"I'm not goin' to abduct her, for Christ sake, John! Just try to mend some fences between us and hope for a date later on."

John put his cigarette out in the ashtray. "I like Sarah. It'll be nice to see her."

"She's coming out now." Orson grinned while opening the car door and scrambling outside. "Wait here, John. Rest your wounded ass. I'll be right back." Orson put his cigarette between his lips and slammed the door shut. John watched him walk quickly to the bunch of waitresses walking out into the cold air through the kitchen door. The lights around the restaurant doors were bright and John could see Orson waving his arm in the air as he closed in on the women. Most of them stopped as Orson approached, but after a second or so, they started walking again towards their cars except for Sarah and another woman. To John's surprise, the two women began walking with Orson. As they came closer into John's view, he could see Sarah had her hair tied up into a ponytail and was pretty well bundled up in winter garments to see any more of her. John lowered the side window as they neared and called out to her, "Hi, good-looking!"

Sarah rushed to the car and reached down inside the open car window hugging as much of John as she could grab while at the same time kissing his cheek.

"See, Sarah," Orson cried out. "I wasn't lying about John being in the car and wanting to see you. Can your watchdog go on her way now? Me and John will give you a ride home."

"Sarah stood erect and turned to the older waitress. "You can go, Doris, everything's fine. I'll ride home with them, but thanks for the offer anyhow."

The woman nodded her head and walked away.

Orson let Sarah and John cuddle and mumble niceties to each other before opening the back door of the car. "Come on, Sarah; get in and out of the cold." Sarah climbed into the back seat and Orson shut it behind her. He rushed around to the driver's side of the car, opened the back door, and jumped inside beside a startled Sarah. Before either

Sarah or John could say a word he quickly began explaining himself. "I just want to talk! Get some things straight between us!"

Sarah turned to open the door and looked to John. "John, what's going on? Are you both drunk?"

Orson grabbed her arm. "Give me a minute, Sarah. What the hell is a minute after what you did to me?"

"I haven't the slightest idea what's goin' on," John turned and stared at them in the back seat. "Orson, get the hell up here in the front and drive!"

"I don't want a ride home!" Sarah yelled and opened the door.

Orson quickly reached across her lap and pulled the door shut, angered at her refusal to even talk with him. "You're not goin' anywhere, Bitch!" He grabbed her by the ponytail. "You're not hiding in your Mommy's house tonight! Drive to River Road, John!"

Sarah yelped.

John reached over and turned the engine off. He took the keys out of the ignition clutching them inside his big fist. He screamed at his cousin who was now trying to force his hands inside of Sarah's heavy clothing. "Let her go, Orson! Now!"

Sarah started screaming. "Help me, John! Help me!"

John opened the car door and started slowly sliding himself outside.

"Stay out of this, John!" Orson barked. "She made an ass out of me, told her girlfriends about it, and now she's gonna pay." Orson slapped her face, manhandling her down onto the seat and started unbuttoning her coat. "We're family, John! Stay out of it." He started ripping her clothes.

John put the car keys into his coat pocket, walked around the car, and opened the back door. He grabbed Orson by the legs and pulled as hard as he could, but Orson mounted Sarah and was clutching her upper body with his arms. Orson braced his one foot against the inside frame of the car.

"Don't be an asshole, John," Orson begged. "You can have some too!"

Sarah was whimpering. John dropped his cousin's legs, reached down between them and grabbed Orson by his erection and testicles and he squeezed hard and gave Orson an opportunity to save his manhood. "Cousin, let her go now or I'll rip your goodies off and drop them in this parking lot for some crow's breakfast. So help me God, I will!" John squeezed harder and gave a threatening yank.

"Okay! Okay!" Orson relinquished mumbling to Sarah as he withdrew from the car. "Bitch!"

John held onto Orson's pride and easily pulled him to the front of the car. He watched Sarah get out of the car and walk away clutching her torn clothing. "Thanks, John," she uttered, sobbing.

"Wait, Sarah," John pleaded. "I'll walk you home." Sarah stopped and waited for John.

John took Orson's car keys from his pocket with his free hand and tossed them on the ground and looked his cousin in the face. "Get some help, Orson. Your head needs a tune up."

"Okay, Dense One," Orson snickered. "Now run and fix her car, kiss her ass, and just maybe she'll give your broken ass some." John pushed him aside and walked to Sarah's side. After they'd walked some distance they heard Orson's loud voice cursing them. He found his keys on the ground, and drove off recklessly, passing fast and close to the cuddling couple.

CHAPTER TEN

By the Fourth of July John, moved into Sarah's apartment. The news got to Tim swiftly by way of Bonnie who became a regular at the Piano Bar when Tim began playing there. He was always being given news about Sarah if he asked for it or not. He always wanted to hear about Sarah, even hearsay, but seldom asked for it. Fitch and Gypsy stopped by the Piano Bar now and then. It was Gypsy, after a few drinks who blurted out to Tim about John's confrontation with his cousin. It must have bothered Gypsy that her Lover was interested in Sarah, because on that particular evening, the mention of Orson's name brought fire into her eyes.

John never stopped by the Piano Bar since his fight with Orson, and neither did Orson. He felt relieved in one way. Sarah would come to no harm from Orson with John around to watch over her. Tim smiled to himself. And he thought he'd gotten over on John with Kimiko.

Bonnie helped him walk out of the Piano Bar. He'd been miserable all evening but he smiled and played the keys, taking every drunken request along with every drink handed to him. He was too drunk to drive to his parent's home. Bonnie loaded him into her bigger car and took him to her apartment where he passed out.

He had a headache. He felt nakedness against him. He opened his eyes to sunlight and Bonnie. "How did I get here?"

They were both lying naked on Bonnie's bed. "I dragged you," Bonnie whispered into his ear. "And then I pulled your clothes off."

"God, my head hurts," he muttered.

"I'll get you some aspirin."

"Please," he begged.

Bonnie lifted herself and sat up beside him. He looked at her small breasts and reached out and touched one.

She smiled down on him. "And you always loved my hair."

Bonnie swung herself off the bed and walked across the room, her light brown hair flowing down her long straight back. She brought the pills and water, leaned over the bed with her breasts close to him. Tim took the pills, swallowed them with difficulty, and laid his head slowly back down onto the soft pillow.

Bonnie climbed onto the bed on her knees and fell back on her haunches.

Tim narrowed his eyes. "It happened between us last night?"

Bonnie giggled. "Sometime between midnight and morn."

Tim looked over her slender body, then into her smiling triumphant eyes. "Christ, Bonnie." He snapped. "You're beautiful!"

Bonnie laughed. "Morning after words I haven't heard before."

CHAPTER ELEVEN

Tim pounded out the customary *Auld Lang Syne* as a sign that it was time to close the bar and a musical signal to the crowd to drink up and go home. He wasn't even close to being as high as he'd been on past Saturday nights at closing time, but he was tired and wanted to get back to the apartment and Bonnie. It was a holiday weekend and the union town of Rivers Bend always celebrated Labor Day with a parade and much merriment afterwards.

It was a loud crowd, pulling silly gags on each other with plenty of would be drunken lounge singers huddling about the piano belching out songs they knew few right words too. This barrage of drunken cheerfulness mixed with slurred words and occasional sprays of spit was giving Brogan a taste of his future if he remained a piano man.

Ben didn't make any move to shut down the bar and continued serving drinks and breaking the law. He had been drinking most of the evening, something he rarely did behind the bar. He was acting irresponsible and it seemed to Tim that he didn't want the evening to end.

Tim finished playing *Auld Lang Syne*, turned on the piano bench, and watched Ben for some sort of hint of his intentions. Ben was talking to a woman, a stranger to Tim. He was laughing, being silly in her company, and acting far outside of his normal character.

Tim played *Auld Lang Syne* again, and again turned on the bench. Ben was still serving drinks, acting foolhardy, with the woman still smiling at him. Brogan waited on the bench, expecting sooner rather than later that Ben would come to his senses and tell all to drink up and go home. He was taking an irrational gamble by violating Commonwealth liquor laws and risking his license to operate.

Ben saw Tim looking his way. He staggered to the piano showing a big smile and carrying a glass of beer in his good hand. He placed the glass on the piano next to Tim's tip plate and leaned close to Tim. "Play some more, Tim. I'm staying open. I'll pay you extra."

"Ben, you'll lose your liquor license."

"Piss on 'em!" He leaned over the piano, his hand slid onto the keyboard. A loud sound shot from the piano. He straightened himself. A goofy looking smile crossed his face and he nodded to the woman stranger. "See that lady at the bar, the stocky one?" Ben didn't wait for

Tim's reply before he slurred out his plans. "I'm gonna invite her to my apartment."

Tim smiled. "Well do it... and let's close this place up."

"I'm not ready yet...play more music."

"Who is she?"

"She's on her way to Erie, her car broke down. It's over at John's garage."

Tim took the glass of cold beer Ben brought him and drank some. "Ben, why lose your license? The state police go by and see you open, that's it, a heavy fine at least."

Ben leaned close to Tim's face. "Piss on it, this is more important to me. Is that guy wearing the baseball hat still by her?"

Tim leaned, looking around Ben's stout body. The guy and lady from Erie were kissing. "Yeah, I see him. Who is he?"

Ben stood up and gave off a low sounding belch. "A steel hauler from Illinois, that's who... picking up a load Monday. "Trying to cut me out."

Tim sighed. "Ben, he's kissing her...and she doesn't seem to mind."

Ben threw up his arm. "That's it! Forget it! Play *Auld Lang Syne.*"

Tim did as the boss said. The intoxicated bodies found their way to the outside and the lady from Erie left with the truck driver.

Tim pocketed his tip money from the plate and said goodnight to Ben. Ben didn't answer and Tim walked over to the bar. "What's wrong?"

Ben turned up the bar lights as bright as they could go. "Just go home...leave me alone. I want to be alone."

Tim leaned on the bar and repeated himself. "What's wrong, Ben?"

Ben dropped a glass and it burst on the floor. "Shit!" He screamed and began kicking the stack of wooden beer cases he used to sit his lumpish body on when business was slow.

Tim thought he'd better leave Ben alone with his anger. "Goodnight, Ben," he said and walked to the open front door. He stepped out into the warm September air and looked back through the doorway at his boss. Ben was gripping a rag, wiping the bar top very fast, staggering around the curves of the horseshoe bar, wiping, knocking bottles, glasses and ashtrays onto the floor.

Tim lit a cigarette and took a deep puff. This was no way to live. He was getting tired of playing the same songs over and over again. Tired of drunks when he was sober. And tired of sobriety when it felt better getting drunk. And most of all, he was tired of people that talked and talked but said so little. He liked his boss, but he needed to change his life.

CHAPTER TWELVE

Tim was on the sofa reading a magazine with his back propped up against two big pillows and listening to Connie Francis when Bonnie came home from work. The same place he was everyday when she came home from work since quitting his job at the piano bar six months ago.

Entering the living room with her kelly green dress unbuttoned in front she kicked off her high heel shoes. With a wide swing of her fist she knocked the magazine from his hands. She slithered onto his lounging body while unsnapping her bra and tossed it across the room. "Are you certain you're not sewn to this sofa?"

Tim chuckled.

Bonnie opened his pajama top. "I better check and see." She wiggled her slim body over him. "I love you, Brogan," she whispered softly.

He put both arms around her and started rubbing her back with one hand and playing with the ends of her long hair with the other. "I love you too, Bonnie."

A pressing kiss by Bonnie sent the back of his head deep into the pillows. Bonnie, breathing hard again, whispered into his ear. "Never stop lying to me, Tim."

"I won't," he answered before he realized what he'd said. "I mean..."

Bonnie jumped up and off of him. She stood over him glaring. "You bastard! Must you be so honest?"

"It was an honest mistake!" Tim shot back at her. "I thought you said never stop loving me!" He started to get up off the sofa.

She shoved him back down and shook her finger at his startled face. Her little breasts were quivering. "Now!" she shouted. "You're absolutely lying!" She strutted away slapped the stereo as she went by it. The music stopped. She fell into an overstuffed chair across the room.

Tim rolled himself up into a sitting position and put on his slippers. He didn't look at Bonnie. He did nothing except support his hanging head with his hands and elbows. There were many minutes of silence between them before Bonnie spoke to him in a commanding way. "I want to go out tonight, to downtown Pittsburgh!"

Brogan mumbled something under his breath.

"Was that oink I just heard …a 'yes Bonnie' or a 'no Bonnie'?" She quizzed.

Brogan lifted his eyes to her and spoke softly. "Suppose to rain."

"That's it!" Bonnie fired more anger at him. "It's raining bullshit now! Did you take weather reports before you took Sarah's ass to Pittsburgh on a Friday night?" She jumped up out of the chair, scooped up her bra and put it back on. "Some people get all the luck. Sarah got nice size tits and now she's getting a nice size you-know-what from John."

Tim lit a cigarette and leaned back into the sofa tilting his head and blowing smoke rings at the ceiling.

Bonnie, after buttoning up the front of her dress, parked herself back onto the overstuffed chair and lit a cigarette. Tim wouldn't quarrel with her and was acting indifferent. She shifted on the chair. They both puffed in silence. The only sounds in the room came from an angrily shifting Bonnie.

It started to rain. Tim turned his head to the window and watched the raindrops splash against the window pane. He annoyed her. "April showers, just as promised."

Bonnie warned him. "Quit being a smartass, Tim or I'll…"

She stopped talking, got out of the chair and went to the small bar. She stood with her back to Tim, mixing herself a drink. He was making light of her and her envy of Sarah, acting like he was above such petty behavior, while all the while moping inside for his lost darling. She took a sip of her strong drink, turned to Tim, and gave him her best feline scorn. She spoke with bitter sweetness in her voice while holding the cocktail glass close to her lips. "Do you think, Tim… that Sarah and her former husband used one of those heart shaped beds on their honeymoon at Niagara Falls?"

Tim puffed on his cigarette and watched the rain fall. He could hear and see the drops splashing against the window.

She sipped and puffed waiting for him to respond to her acidic question. He quietly sat watching the storm and puffing on his cigarette.

She moved in front of him and dropped her still burning cigarette butt into the ashtray he held in his hand. Tim inhaled a whiff of her perfumed scent; saw her manicured and long polished fingernails moving away. He crushed out her butt.

"I heard Sarah and John are getting hitched soon. Have you heard anything? It's probably all rumor. I wonder if she'll go back to Niagara again." Bonnie made a contemptuous sound. "I hope she has the decency not to make love in the same heart shaped bed she used with her first husband. Naaa…I don't think she would. Johnny Boy is a lot bigger... needs a lot more room...if you know what I mean, Timmy." Bonnie showed him the pleasing look on her face and swung her long legs over the arm of the chair.

Tim crushed his cigarette out and placed the ashtray on the floor. He went to the bar, poured himself a mouthful of straight whiskey and bolted it down his throat with his back to Bonnie. He poured himself another.

Bonnie jumped to her feet. "That's right! Get stoned! Numb your Sarah memories. Kill your mind! Why don't you just get a gun and blow your head off?"

Tim turned to her while raising his voice. "I'm not talking about Sarah...you are! I never talk about Sarah, yet each time I annoy you...you do. You have the Sarah problem...not me!"

Bonnie moved close to his face. "You're right! I hate her!" She flopped back into the chair.

Tim sat on the sofa arm. "For heaven's sake, Bonnie, give me a break. All that I said was, or meant was, that I didn't want to drive to Pittsburgh in the rain."

"Why not? You can't be tired. You don't do anything all day long except lie around moping and listening to music."

"Not after tonight. You broke the stereo." Tim sighed. "Okay, let's go to Pittsburgh."

She shifted in the chair. "You sound enthused."

Tim finished his drink and went to the bar and put his glass down. "I want to go, Bonnie. I didn't before, but now I want to go to Pittsburgh with you."

She stared at him wearing his pajamas and began to feel sorry for him. "I'm sorry. I don't hate Sarah. Just somewhat jealous of her."

"Forget about it," he said. "We all vent our woes sometime, somehow, on someone, in someway."

Bonnie lit up another cigarette and motioned for the ashtray. Tim stooped and shoved it across the hardwood floor to her. She took the ash holder in one hand. "I get upset too easily."

He spoke to her softly. "Bonnie, I do love you."

"But not like Sarah. Tim, you will never get over her or forgive her for betraying you. I think you just use me."

"If so, you let me, but I do love you. We did so much together growing up and in high school. Our lives are knotted together like two ropes and no matter what our future turns out to be, I will always love you, Bonnie."

Bonnie toned down her anger as easily as she had escalated it. She lived in fear that someday Tim would walk out of her life. If only she could keep her envy over Sarah under control, she might someday dare get her hopes high and have him for the rest of her life. She sat the ashtray on the floor and started to cry, covering her face with both hands.

Tim went to her and took her by the hands and pulled her up into his arms, cradling her head against his chest. He kissed the top of her head. "Bonnie," he whispered. "We'll take the incline up to Mount Washington, enjoy a candlelit dinner, and if it stops raining, take a river boat cruise. How does that sound?"

Mumbling something, she put her arms around his waist whimpering. She was frail against his brawny body and after a while went silent standing inside of his smothering arms, not wanting and unable to fight anymore. He picked her up and carried her to the bedroom.

CHAPTER THIRTEEN

The rectory was warm.

Father Eugene met Tim at the rear door and helped the exhausted missionary with his coat and hung it on a rack behind the door. The old priest was lecturing him as if Tim were one of his regular altar boys. "Thank the Good Lord you made it to Saint James safely. I was worried and I prayed for you all night long. Driving in that storm! You couldn't wait it out before coming to Rivers Bend? Gosh, Tim! I know you're feeling pain over your two friends, but you don't have to kill yourself, too!"

Tim led the way to the kitchen, the old priest close behind. "Well, your prayers were heard and I am delivered into your hands for a few hours. Then I'm heading back to New York."

Tim waited for the reaction from his childhood pastor.

"Timothy! You need more than a few hours. Hells-spells, you'll kill yourself. There's a shortage of priests as it is! And besides, you look like hell!"

Tim chuckled. "You're the second person to tell me."

"Go upstairs and get some sleep and we'll talk about this driving madness later." Father Eugene waved his hands at the younger priest. "Shoo now, get upstairs!"

Brogan's wet shoes squeaked on the tile floor and louder while climbing the wooden stairs. The guest bedroom was small, bright and painted white. A small crucifix hung on the wall above the bed.

Tim stripped off his outer clothing and sat in his underwear on the edge of the sturdy single bed. His trousers and shirt, shoes and socks lay crumpled in a pile on the floor. He was too worn out to pick them up and fold them. He needed to take a shower, but he forgot to bring his suitcase along from the car. He was too tired to dress and too cozy to go back outside into the cold to get it.

The short uncomfortable nap at the funeral home had taken the edge off his exhaustion and although he needed more sleep, his racing mind would not allow it.

Lying on his back, he looked up at the crucifix, thinking of Sarah. He wished he would have married her. He stretched his wish. Why couldn't he be living the perfect life? A missionary priest and Sarah's husband? What was this creed he lived by? This mixture of Middle East Judaic beliefs and Roman traditions. Peter was married, Paul was not.

Why not Tim? Christ, in choosing Peter to lead the twelve, addressed the position clearly. He didn't care that Peter was married! Why was he suffering since the day he was ordained for a woman, a mate, a Sarah? Was it only because bishops of olden days misused their authority, persuading kings to appoint their son's to succeed themselves, and thereby keeping the church lands and treasures in their families? The church's holy solution to stop such abuse of power…celibacy!

What were the modern reasons for a celibate priesthood? None that mattered under close examination to Tim. The world is smaller now in 1984. Communications around the world, superb. Rome appoints bishops, not kings. If the need ever existed for a celibate priesthood, the time had passed. He had been celibate since living with Bonnie and at middle age he had no desire for intimacy with every woman he passed in life. But he did have desire.

He rolled onto his stomach. He loved Bonnie, too, but in a different way than Sarah. He liked being in her company. It was Bonnie that got him off the piano stool and nursed him through months of drunkenness after John moved in with Sarah. Bonnie was always there for him. Got him to quit drinking himself into an insensible state. She fed him. She cleaned his clothes. How else could he have survived working at the Piano Bar? Remarks made by men about Bonnie's sexual permissiveness when Tim was at the Piano Bar were better said in whispers or face acid remarks from Brogan about their own shortcomings.

Tim crushed his pillow up and buried his face into its softness. How did that happen? Characterizing only women by their sexual past? Men gloat when their bride is a virgin, while a woman is plain happy to marry a man she loves.

Tim let go of the pillow and crawled under the covers thinking that if he got warm enough he'd fall asleep. Sleep that he needed, but his churning mind would not let him have without a struggle to release its thoughts. She's a whore, God, because I had to pay her, but I'm still a man. She's a slut, God, because I seduced her too easily, but I'm still a man. She's a pig, God, because, because, because… but I'm still a man. She is good, God, because she is a virgin, but I remain a man regardless of what I do sexually.

Tim shuddered or shivered beneath the heavy blanket, he didn't know which. Was it any wonder that Jesus warned that the prostitutes will see the kingdom of heaven before the hypocrites? Was Christ speaking of the men that called Bonnie nasty names in their younger years when he said that nothing that goes into the body defiles it, only what comes out?

Tim pulled the covers over his head, shutting out the morning sunlight. But he was still thinking of Bonnie. She never married and wrote to him wherever he was in the world. Should he call her before he left town? On his previous visits to Rivers Bend over the years he had met Bonnie in the City Park. They talked, laughed, fed the pigeons, and enjoyed each other's company. But that is as far as Tim would allow the relationship to go, only talk with small hugs. But Bonnie always hinted she would like more to pass between them than pigeon feed on his short visits home. In his present mindset it would be dangerous to call Bonnie. Dangerous to his vow of celibacy. After seeing Sarah's corpse, his life of self-sacrifice was losing its grip on his soul.

Why struggle if it wasn't required? In his heart, he wanted to do more than call Bonnie. He wanted Bonnie to take care of him now in his sorrow, as she took care of him before when his mind and body both seemed alone and forgotten in his world of nothing. He wanted to feel alive. He wanted to feel a woman. He wanted to be in love. He couldn't run to Sarah, Sarah was dead. He could run to Bonnie. He could always run to easy Bonnie. Many men ran to easy Bonnie. She was lonely too.

Tim rolled into a fetal position in the warm darkness of his cocoon. Let's all go and stone Bonnie. Why wasn't a man beside the adulteress in the Bible story? Why didn't the adulterer also fear for his life from the self righteous mob about to stone the woman to death? Would Jesus have forgiven that man as quickly as he did the woman? Did Jesus know something that we are never told in the story? Could she have been skinny? Bones alone? Ignorant? Poor? Even ugly and not appealing and shameful looking as the Renaissance painters presented her to us? Perhaps a trade off, gimme sex, little woman, for food to feed your children? Where was that adulterer? In the mob with a rock in his hand shouting death to Bony Bonnie! Jesus forgave the adulteress; it's not recorded what the message was that he wrote in the sand with his finger. Did it instruct the woman to forgive the hypocrites with rocks in their paws? Or, did the message say "I know why you are sinning, to feed your children, and I forgive you." But, then again, perhaps the adulteress was a beautiful and selfish bitch that broke her family's heart. And if she was unrepentant, would Jesus' admonition to her still only be to go and sin no more?

Would Jesus forgive him for speaking to Sarah in a forgiving and understanding way for the pain she had brought into his life, but within his mind detesting her decision to write him off for another? Did he really leave her because it was for their own good or to get back at her?

At this moment Brogan only knew that he'd risk gambling his soul with demons if he could go back to that morning he left her bed and tell her he would never leave her again. Stupid! That's what he was! He bounced his head up and down into the crushed pillow. Stupid! Stupid! Stupid! He called himself stupid until he started dozing off into a dreamy state of mind.

He jerked his face from the pillow. His heart was racing. His misty thought of Bonnie seemed real, the smooth pillow Bonnie's flesh. He had to stop torturing himself. He got up out of bed, walked to the window and looked out over snow covered Rivers Bend.

The roads were clear. Traffic was moving without delay, but the wind still howled, blowing snow into big drifts that would last throughout the winter before melting. He could see the Ohio. Ice chunks were floating in the river.

The steel mill was still the dominant structure in town, but the priest knew that times were different than in the sixties. Rivers Bend suffered high unemployment. The mill's operational days were numbered and when the steel breadbox quit providing work, Rivers Bend would turn stale and crumble.

Tim could see that the town fell further along into its downhill slide since his last visit. Roads were not maintained and most potholes left unfilled. Small businesses near the mill were closed or closing. Building fronts were being boarded up with plywood. The young people were leaving or thinking of leaving town, no longer able to put their school books down, walk to the mill and go to work for a good wage. Tim could see the bridge crossing the Ohio. Beyond the span, the countryside was hilly and sparsely populated. The bridge road connected to the interstate that the young used to get on the fast track and away from Rivers Bend.

The window rattled from a strong burst of gusty wind. The window was old. It needed to be replaced. Saint James collection basket was also suffering from Rivers Bend financial troubles. Tim smiled to himself. He could never get a satisfying answer from anyone why the town name referred to more than one river. There was only one river with one bend.

Tim drew some musical notes in the condensation on the windowpane. Straight below the pane he could see the snow covered City Park. It spread out in front of the church grounds. In all four seasons he had walked Sarah through that park. They fed the pigeons and squirrels, and built a snowman for little Lynn. In the park, Sarah wrote in the snow with a tree twig. "Sarah loves Tim."

And what about Lynn? At first after being ordained on his brief visits home, he never went to John and Sarah's home. At Bonnie's urging, he went to John's garage to say hello and hoped that John would call Sarah and tell her he was in town. For many years he only spoke to her by phone from the garage after John would hand him the receiver with his big greasy hand. The conversations were never as long as Tim would hope, but what else was proper to say after the niceties were said and done? Then one time he was surprised when Sarah came to the garage and brought him and John lunch.

After years away in Central America and many letters to John and Sarah about his work, he was invited by letter for dinner whenever he came home. The visits to their home were always awkward for him and eventually he and John would end up reminiscing about things in their past that really didn't mean much to either one of them. By then, Lynn was in high school. Tim knew by the warm friendly letters Sarah sent to him that Lynn, after graduating from college entered the Navy. He wished he would have gotten to know Lynn better.

Brogan pressed his face several different ways against the cold glass pane hoping to get a glimpse of the apartment where he had lived with Sarah. He could see a bounty of old houses looking picturesque adorned with fresh white snow, but he could not see the apartment building and felt cheated.

He lifted his arm to scratch himself and the smell coming from his armpits sent him to his pile of wet clothes. He dressed and went outside into the cold to fetch his belongings. After more than twenty years, he was still full of uncertainties. Still questioning himself. Could he have married Sarah without Mr. Murky being their best man?

After a hot shower and several swipes of deodorant, he felt much better. He still looked tired, but not old and weary. He shaved, brushed his teeth, put on clean underwear and got underneath the covers to find sleep. Spongy memories of Sarah and Bonnie mixed with John and Orson and others from his youth danced in his head. His thoughts began to slow and his body unwound. Tim slipped into sleep.

Brogan woke up to bells ringing. He sat up in bed. He was groggy and his eyes could not focus. The room was shadowy. He felt for the lamp and turned it on. He answered the telephone. Father Eugene told him it was time for supper and that he had a message from Fitch.

He dressed slowly. The room was full of musty smells. He went to the window and opened it to the winter air, diluting the smells, getting a chill over his tall lean body. He shut the window but stood gazing through the icy pane into the night and lights of Rivers Bend. He slept too long. He would wait until early morning to drive back to the seminary. He headed for the kitchen. And what did Fitch want?

After supper, Tim took the after dinner cigar Father Eugene gave him but decided against smoking it so the white wool sweater he wore didn't smell of smoke. Tim seldom smoked anymore, but there were times when he gave himself over to the urge of nicotine. After a bit of conversation with his old friend and pastor, Tim returned to his bedroom.

    He sat on the unmade bed, leaned forward, and fiddled with the cigar. He sat the cigar on the nightstand under the dim lamplight. He had to squint to look at his watch. Almost seven. He would have to go into the church. Fitch would be coming.

CHAPTER FOURTEEN

The funeral home was crowded. The parishioners from Saint James and the citizens of Rivers Bend came in a swarm to pay their respects to John and Sarah's families causing many problems for the undertaker. The parking lot was full. Drivers began parking on the narrow street, and up onto the sidewalks. A line of people, wrapped for winter's weather, formed throughout the corridor. In the hallway, the undertaker kept coffee brewing for the shivering visitors who were offering their condolences to Lynn.

Dutch approached John's coffin and bowed his head. At middle age and carrying a potbelly, few of his clothes fit him anymore. Seldom did he have an occasion to wear a suit of clothes, so he refused to buy one, thinking it financially unsound.

Being a practical man, measuring life with greenbacks, Dutch found John's death worrisome. To have so much going in your favor monetarily and then to pass on was sickening. John's garage business was never better. Fewer people bought new cars since the massive layoffs at the mill, and the uncertain future for those fortunate enough to be still working made them cautious and fearful of making long term financial contracts. Steel mill workers were now doing what Dutch had always done, repairing their car over and over again instead of rushing to buy a new car every few years.

Sarah's daughter had greeted him when he entered the room. It occurred to Dutch that her commitment to the Navy could possibly incline her to take a hasty and cheap price for John's new house that now belonged to her.

Dutch moved to Sarah's coffin, and joining that thought about John's new house was another, one with an opportunity to make money. Dutch wondered if Lynn would also sell off John's garage and tools cheaply. A small business on the side could be a wise investment with the mill slowing down. The garage would be money-making security. A little treasure to increase the numbers in his bank account. With unemployment high, he could hire a mechanic to work cheap, too. Of course, he would have to be less cavalier with his pricing than John was, who often adjusted his prices to help the many down on their luck. He turned from Sarah's corpse and went to Lynn.

Orson lingered close to a wall, near some flowers and ferns, his handsome facial features somber below a thinning crop of hair. His body remained trim and muscular beneath his dark gray suit. He looked over at Sarah's coffin. He couldn't see her face, only parts of her light brown dress. Too many people crowded her corpse.

Sarah continued being a temptation to him when he would see her shapely body sauntering around Rivers Bend. She always looked much younger than her age. He always wanted revenge for what she had done to him. Sitting inside his car that long-ago night full of anticipation, wanting and waiting, only to be turned away through trickery. She made him a joke. He could still picture her peeping at him through the curtains of the front window, safe inside her parents' house.

Someone in the crowd of women around Sarah's body began to sob. Orson looked over at Lynn in her naval uniform and felt a surge of lust to feed his wanton fancies. He didn't know how to halt his yearning thoughts for Lynn, he only knew how to nurse them along...coveting came easy to him.

Orson could see some of Sarah's features in Lynn like her radiant green eyes, but her hair was lighter than her mother's and it had a bouncy softness to it that he longed to touch. Her uniform fit her perfectly. Her long legs...he shook his head, shuddered, and turned his eyes back to Sarah's body before moving closer to Lynn.

The line was moving slowly. Gypsy longed for a cigarette. She had come to the funeral home hoping to find Fitch, but discovered that he had already been there and left. She was uneasy about new developments in their long marriage. She had never been a proper wife for Fitch, but he always tolerated her drunkenness and unfaithfulness. Seldom did they fight about her behavior anymore, and that is why his sudden plans to leave her were so shocking. Fitch's early retirement from the mill left him financially free to go. He threatened to leave her before, but she always correctly guessed he was only bluffing. She spotted Orson across the room. He was talking to Lynn, giving her his big smile.

Gypsy looked herself over; her blue winter coat was old, and a bit too small. She couldn't recall the last time Orson called upon her. Orson didn't like pudgy women. Nowadays she wasn't known for being Fitch's unfaithful wife or Orson's lover, just Gypsy, who smokes and drinks too much and looks much older than her age.

She hadn't seen Fitch since that morning when he told her he was leaving and going to Arizona to live with their son. He said that his flight left that night and he already had his luggage packed. She didn't love her husband, but she would miss him. She was fond of Fitch; he was the only stable part of her life. For Fitch's sake, she wanted to feel some remorse for making his life so miserable, but regret for sleeping with Orson was beyond her abilities. She was just too much of a selfish person to allow other people's feelings to stop her from acting out her desires. Orson could still take her at any time with his big smile; that smile that Sarah's daughter was now facing.

She needed a smoke. Why was she in this line anyhow? After Sarah married John, she seemed to be wrapped up with being a wife and mother and church worker at Saint James...a place Gypsy wouldn't go to seek friends. So why was she standing in this long line? To see a corpse that she had hardly seen very much of when it was alive over the past twenty years? Fitch had sent flowers in both of their names... good enough! Gypsy stepped out of line and rushed outside into the cold night, lit up an unfiltered and trudged to the corner bar.

CHAPTER FIFTEEN

Sitting in the dark nave, Tim gazed at the scantily lit sanctuary, the white marble altar, the candles, and fresh cut flowers from the last row of pews. Beyond the altar, the statues of Saint James and Saint Joseph faced out over the nave, perched inside lancet openings built into the front stone wall of the church.

He looked below the side altar where the nativity scene was traditionally erected at Christmastime. He remembered himself as a boy and how he marveled at the images of the three wise men and their camels. How those majestic travelers charged his imagination and set him off daydreaming about also going to faraway places, to exotic lands, meeting strange people and seeing strange worlds just as the gift bearers.

He stared down the center aisle. Sarah had walked down that aisle to a waiting and excited Mr. Murky. Now inside her casket she would be pushed on a gurney down that same aisle and once again he would be far away from Rivers Bend.

Father Eugene had welcomed Sarah back to Saint James after she married John. Sarah had written Tim that the old priest had made a special effort to make her feel wanted since she married John outside of the church and could not receive communion.

An annulment of her first marriage, she had written to Tim, with annulment underlined as if to remind him of their long ago discussion on that subject, would be of small use since John, as a declared unbeliever, refused to believe in any God for the sake of a church wedding. Further on in that same letter, Sarah confessed that she too still believed as Tim did about annulments. What was done, she wrote, cannot be undone with tricky vocabulary.

Tim shuffled in the pew. It angered him that Sarah or anyone would be refused communion. Communion for Sarah would have been comforting to her, a sort of self-indulgence in hope after being rash and foolish in youth. To deny Sarah Eucharist was to restrict hope and perhaps even forbid hope to embrace her spirit.

A better way, he believed, would be for the church to have an open policy on communion and not use it as a menacing holy club over the heads of those that fall short of Jesus' teaching on divorce. Welcoming all sinners to Christ's table would be more equitable than being a sifter of sinners to see who is worthy of Eucharist. Even Judas broke bread with Christ at the last Supper without having his hand slapped by Jesus. Tim hated divorce but believed it would be better to stand at heaven's gate dripping with guilt over a selfish divorce than being at the gate dressed in the costume of make believe, the cloth of annulment.

Tim heard a faint noise. It was Fitch crossing himself. Brogan laid the stole in his hand on the pew beside him.

Fitch slid into the pew next to Tim. The two friends shook hands. Fitch's camel hair overcoat made him appear broader in the shoulders.

Tim asked in a low voice. "You said you wanted to go to confession, Fitch? To me? Is there a particular reason why you asked for me over regular reconciliation hours with Father Eugene?"

Fitch nodded his head. "A couple. There are a few things I think you should know before I leave town," Fitch paused then added, "for good."

"Forever?" Tim questioned.

"Yeah," Fitch mumbled.

"Where are you going? Is Gypsy going too?"

"I'm leaving Gypsy, Tim. I stayed with her for the kid's sake... and my job, playing her and Orson's chump. What else could I do?"

"Where are you going?"

"Arizona. To live with my son. I have to leave soon for Pittsburgh International, so listen to me, Tim, and don't think what I say is just an attempt to get back at Orson."

Tim took his old friend's hand. "I wouldn't do that, Fitch. I know how much embarrassment you suffered over the years. You did the right and honorable thing by staying with your children."

Fitch dropped his head, his eyes were watering up. "No one ever gave me any credit for hanging in there. Thanks, Tim," he mumbled, "it means a lot to me."

"What's this about Orson?" Brogan asked.

"He's going to make a run for Lynn, Tim!" Fitch raised his voice. "I know it. I know him like the back of my hand. He's gone over the edge. Bonkers! And Lynn doesn't have a John around to protect her."

"How do you know this?"

"I was at the funeral home early this afternoon. Few people were there. I gave Lynn my condolences and just hobnobbed for a while. When she told me how attentive, as she put it, Orson has been, helping her get through her crisis, I was suspicious. I've known him too long. 'He's up to no good,' I said to myself. When Orson came into the parlor a few minutes later and heard him being praised, he knew I wasn't being taken in and gave me that, 'so what's it to you?' look. I just want to tell someone, someone that can warn her about him, someone she'll believe. You know, Tim, underneath that phony front Orson puts on, the let 'bygones be gone' crap, he hated Sarah and John. Behind their backs he called them all sorts of names. He called them, ahh...I don't wanta say in church. But you know it was about John's wound from Nam."

"Tell me." Tim blurted out.

"Ahh...he'd call them, ahh...Sarah C. Batteries and John Gone-O."

Tim's mind didn't register Fitch's message. "What are you saying? I don't understand."

Fitch waved his hand. "You know, John's wound."

"What about John's wound?"

"John, he wore a bag, you know, had, had his, you know, parts injured, blown off, or something. I'm not sure what the problem was and I never asked him about it."

Fitch was talking but Tim's body slumped in the pew.

"...worked with Orson over twenty years at the mill, and from punching in time to punching out time it was talk, talk, talk, talk, about sex and rotten women. For years I kept my mouth shut, I didn't want to make things worse than they were for me, but I knew when my back was turned he told the guys at work about getting to Gypsy over..."

Tim patted Fitch's hand.

"...got my early pension from the mill secured and I'm outta here."

Tim asked in a low whisper. "Where is Lynn staying in town?"

"She's safe for now, staying with one of Sarah's sisters. It's after the funeral he'll make his move. I think he's going to help her pack some of John and Sarah's personal belongings at the new house. I heard him tell her that he could get plenty of boxes, for her not to worry." Fitch was fiddling with his gloves. Tim patted the nervous Fitch's shoulder. "Quit worrying, Fitch, I'll take care of it."

"I'm nervous about something else too, Tim." Fitch looked downcast. "I never flew before. I'm scared. I want to go to confession."

Tim picked up the folded stole, like a robot, unfolded it, hung it around his neck, crossed it over his sweater, over his breast and waited for Fitch to begin confessing.

After Fitch was finished confession, he sighed in relief. He looked old and tired to Tim. His agonizing life of sharing his wife with Orson wore his body down. Fitch was saying goodbye to Tim forever.

"...never see you again, Tim."

They hugged and with teary eyes, Fitch slid his backside along the pew and left his old friend, his old church, his hometown.

After Fitch had left the church, a stunned Tim stumbled up the center aisle and sat down on the steps of the sanctuary, his mind twisting inside of his skull. He remembered Sarah on the bed crying over his departure, and when he shut the bedroom door on mercy, she settled for gentle John and making a nice life for the crippled Marine and Lynn. Did she sacrifice herself away and decide to live on memories just as he did when he walked into the seminary? He didn't know the answer to that question, and deep down inside himself, he didn't want to know.

Tim's eyes darted around the nave; at the stained glass windows, the statues, the front pews, where he and Orson had sat along with Sarah and Bonnie, Dutch and John, Fitch and others, learning about God, learning prayers, and learning how to be good to one another. It was time wasted on Orson, but not on John.

John was angry at God, not at his teachings. Angry at God for the pain his Mother brought to him as a boy, seeing an abomination that shattered his still infantile faith. Blaming the all-powerful God for not preventing the horror he witnessed of his mother and her lover making out while his Daddy was dying in another part of the house. After all, if God is all-powerful, he could have prevented the pain. How does a human get back at the Almighty? With the only weapon available to mankind... deny His existence.

John had rescued Sarah at the restaurant from his cousin's lust. John had kept Sarah safe, making the Orson-types of the world cower down before his protective nature, his forgiving and understanding ways. Kimiko knew she had a white knight when she took John as a protective lover against the long-at-sea sailors, out on the town to feast themselves on a Sodom and Gomorrah menu.

Brogan felt flushed. He wiped his brow. Sweat came off in his palm. He felt weak, dizzy, confused, angry, and guilty. Where was God? Could it be that he was serving an illusion? A myth dreamed up by ancient Jews wandering around a desert? Was he no more than another pagan priest serving yet another false god? What did these symbols mean, these stone-faced statues, colored glass windows, candles? Did they help or hinder faith? Why was he here searching for God and why was Orson not sitting beside him?

Tim bent his head to his knees and closed his eyes. He was too weary to wrestle with God, too perplexed to argue the case of warm colorful ritual, symbols, and images versus the cold, stark, artless way to better find a path to salvation.

Now all he wanted from God was that there is, in the plan of creation, a reason why people turn out with different degrees of faith after being exposed to the same Christian influence. What set him apart from Orson? Orson from John? John from Tim? What God? What? Unless you're not there, God? Unless it's all in the genes.

He pressed his face into his knees. Folded his arms over the top of his head and squeezed hard, crushing the unwanted thoughts that he could be no more than a stooge to an ancient people's imagination, and their attempt to explain to themselves the wonder of all that existed. An illusion handed down to him and reinforced by parents and church while he sat in these pews as a child.

In his mind's eye, he could see himself and the others kneeling in the pews watching a youthful Father Eugene at the altar, bowing. He could see the beauty of the Mass, hear the Latin, hear Orson's words, coarse words too soon for his age, and feel Orson elbowing him, hitting his arm, hissing sounds coming out of the side of Orson's mouth.

"Psst, Tim..."

Tim kept his hands folded in prayer, ignoring Orson. Listening to Father Eugene.

"...Gloria in excelsis..."

Orson elbowed him again.

"...Benedicimus te..."

The watchdog, Sister Mary Pius, a few pews behind them, kept one eye on the rowdy boys of the seventh grade and one eye on the Mass.

"What?" Tim whispered out of the side of his mouth. Not moving his head. Not moving his eyes. Looking straight ahead at Father Eugene.

"...Adoramus te..."

Orson snickered, "Find Bonnie's ass."

Tim scanned the pew of girls in front of him, found Bonnie kneeling beside Sarah, both displaying piety, looking angelic, following Father Eugene's movements at the altar.

"...Agnus Dei...Filius Patris..."

Bonnie's head was six inches higher than Sarah's, her arms bent at the elbow looking like snapped tooth picks. Her cotton pink dress fell from the back of her neck to her skinny bent legs as if filled with nothing.

"Can't find it, can ya? She got no ass."

Tim looked at Sarah's blue and white dress forming into her waist, over her hips, flowing to her legs.

Father Eugene was kissing the altar. "...Dominus vobiscum..."

Orson elbowed Tim again. Giggled. "I told you."

"...Et cum spritu tuo..."

John, kneeling somewhere behind them, whispered his warning. "Here she comes."

Tim and Orson froze, hardly breathing. Sister Pius was at the end of their row of pews pointing her bony finger at them...

Tim unwound his arms from around his head, struggled to his feet and headed to the rectory and Father Eugene's liquor cabinet. He selected a bottle of cheap whiskey, grabbed a glass, matches, and an ashtray, and went to his bedroom.

The dim bedside lamp was still on. The moonlight coming through the window was brighter. Tim turned off the lamp. He sat on the edge of the bed and placed his treasured catch from downstairs on the carpeted floor in front of him. He poured himself a drink. The whiskey hit his throat and made his eyes water. He could feel its warmth go into his stomach. He lit the cigar. The flickering flame from the match illuminated the puffs of smoke being blown from his mouth. He could feel his muscles begin to relax. He poured himself another.

He would have to deal with Orson. He gulped his second drink, poured himself another and walked to the window. Traffic was moving well, beams of light piercing the darkness above the wet streets, fuzzy streaks floating around Rivers Bend came to him through the moist pane. He sipped his drink and puffed his cigar. The glow of the ash reflected in the pane. He could see Bonnie's apartment building across the park. He wanted to call her. See her. Feel her. He needed conversation, the company of a witty woman. At Bonnie's side, he found relief from desiring Sarah before, and now he wanted to be with her again in his new found grief. He fought off the urge to call her with a big puff of smoke.

Maybe the monks of olden days were correct. A man could only meditate on the wonders of God through retreat from the world and its wicked ways. Away from people, away from corruption, away from temptation. Only then could one follow the example of the three monkeys...hear no evil...see no evil...speak no evil.

Brogan drank from his glass and puffed hard. If cigars were around in the time of Jesus, would Christ have smoked one now and then like he drank wine now and then? Tim sipped and chuckled doing a Groucho Marx imitation. "Got a light, Peter?" He was feeling better.

The telephone rang. He rushed to the telephone hoping it was Bonnie. He listened intently before speaking.

"Lynn, I'll do whatever you desire." He offered her his condolences and hung up the phone.

He sat back down on the edge of the bed and refilled his glass. He took a big gulp and swallowed hard. He wouldn't be leaving in the morning after all. Lynn asked him to say John and Sarah's funeral Mass. He puffed and glanced up at the hanging Christ above the bed and mumbled to Him through the hazy smoke. "If there is nothing after this life...I just as well would've skipped it...How about you, Jesus?"

CHAPTER SIXTEEN

Along with the altar boys and the Lector, Father Tim waited inside the red doors of Saint James Church. The tall teen holding the processional cross looked bored leaning on its staff. The group waited in silence for the funeral party to arrive. Some of the altar boys were fidgeting with their vestments, the energy of youth finding it hard to stand still. The lad that was holding the burning candle looked out the small window in the door, giving a weather report.

"It's snowing." Except for the noises caused by the boys shuffling about, the group waited without speaking for the coffins to be brought to the church doors.

Tim would meet the bodies at the door. The coffins would be draped in a pall, recalling Sarah and John's baptism in Christ. Tim was keenly aware that some in the church would dislike a body of a non-believer being welcomed with a blessing. Every church had its purist, even the apostles whom Paul had argued against concerning the rite of circumcision. The boy holding the candle startled Tim from his thoughts.

"They're here, Father."

Tim wore a green chasuble. In the liturgical colors of the church, green symbolized spring over winter, life over death.

The boys pushed the big red doors of Saint James open to the gusty February air. The pallbearers had already placed the caskets on church trucks and started pushing John and Sarah's caskets through the falling snow to the church entrance.

Father Brogan stepped forward and stood under the stone lancet archway to greet the mourners. He had no trouble finding Lynn in the crowd. She was wearing her naval uniform.

Lynn walked around the coffins and embraced Tim. Her face looked tired. Her green eyes sad. Tim kissed her on the forehead. They did not speak.

Tim waited and watched Lynn step away from him and the coffins, joining her aunts and their families. Some mourners began walking around the caskets, going inside the church and out of the cold, while others waited with the bodies for Tim to begin the blessing.

Brogan glanced over the crowd. He could see Orson and Dutch, and Bonnie bundled up in a heavy white hooded coat far back in the crowd.

She had the hood pulled over her head. Tim stepped forward sprinkling holy water on Sarah's coffin.

"I bless the body of Sarah..."

Tim could hear sobs coming from the crowd.

Father Tim moved to John's coffin and repeated the prayer. John had been baptized, attended Saint James School, and was more understanding toward people than Tim was himself. Brogan had no troubles justifying John's blessing, and reminding the people that from birth to death we all belong to God whether we're mad at him or not.

Tim finished the prayers and stepped back. The altar boys spread open the white palls and held them against the caskets until the doors slammed shut against the winds of winter. Brogan said the words of faith.

"On the day of their baptism, John and Sarah put on Christ..."

The rest of the people began filing into the church. When all were seated, Father Tim nodded to the tall teen holding the staff that then raised the cross high. The lad holding the burning candle took his position at the head of John's coffin and the Lector raised the Bible up in front of her for all to see the word of God.

The organ sounded. John's journey down the aisle began. The aisle John had not walked since he was a lad. Tim began singing in a voice above the others, singing the beautiful words of *On Eagle's Wings*. The procession reached the beginning of the sanctuary. John's casket was positioned in front of the main altar.

Father Tim returned to the back of the church. The organist continued playing, the mourners singing. Tim stood by Sarah's coffin. He let out a loud sigh, tears swelling up in his eyes. Today was Valentine's Day.

He began singing, but his mind lost the flow of the words and everything was blurry in front of him. Sarah was beside John, the Mass began. Father Tim bowed at the foot of the altar, praying. After finishing his prayers, he walked up the three steps to the altar.

Facing the mourners, Tim bent, kissed the altar, stood erect, and offered greeting to those assembled.

"The grace of our Lord Jesus Christ..."

Tim continued with his greeting, searching the faces in the pews. He spotted Orson behind Lynn, sitting in the pew with the rest of John's family. Sarah's family was in the front row of pews.

Tim finished his greeting, went and sat in the chair facing the nave. The Lector walked to the pulpit and began the first reading. A woman. Tim did not know her well.

Brogan lowered his eyes. He recalled bringing Sarah a heart-shaped box of candy. It was near Valentine's Day that Sarah had carved in the snow, confirming her love for him, words that melted, a vanishing Valentine.

Brogan sat slumped in the chair praying to God for the courage to get him through the day, this hour of heartbreak. Soon he, too, would be standing at the pulpit. He would keep his words comforting for Sarah and John's families, not shouting the truth that a snake was amongst them pondering ways to use the tragedy in their lives to satisfy his own wickedness.

Bonnie, sitting in one of the middle rows of pews, was remembering Sarah also. The day Sarah had made a surprise visit to her apartment. It was a few years after Tim's ordination and he had gone to Central America. It was before noon on a Sunday and Bonnie was still in her housecoat. Sarah was wearing a fuzzy red sweater. They were having coffee in Bonnie's small kitchen. Sarah was sitting across from her looking sad, but beautiful.

Sarah poured cream into her coffee cup and stirred it slowly, watching the spoon handle go round and round. She lifted her eyes to Bonnie.

"I'm sorry for coming without calling first. I just came from Mass and I was thinking of you and... Well, you live just across the park, close, I guess I was here before I thought much about it."

Bonnie lit a cigarette. "You were thinking of me?"

Sarah smiled. "Bonnie, I know we were never the best of friends in high school, but no bad feelings ever passed between us either. I was never in any clique either. I just sort of quietly went about my business."

Bonnie chuckled. Blew smoke away from Sarah's face. "Sarah, you didn't need to be in any clique. Just by walking the halls you were noticed. To draw half that much attention to myself, I would've had to fall down with at least a main artery gushing blood."

Sarah gave Bonnie a shy smile. "A lot of girls didn't like me, Bonnie. They thought I was stuck up, but I wasn't. I was shy back then. I used to admire you, still do."

Bonnie crushed her cigarette out in a big glass ashtray on the kitchen table. "Me? For what?"

"For the way you were." Sarah folded her hands on her lap. "Still are. Bold, how you performed on stage. Not afraid. You didn't care what the other girls thought of you. What anybody thought of you."

Bonnie sipped her coffee and smiled. "I cared, Sarah." Bonnie lit another cigarette, puffed hard on it. "You know how I was talked about? How easy with the boys I was? It's all true. What wasn't said is that until I was in the eleventh grade, I was never asked out on a date. Then a senior, without mentioning names, asked me to a drive-in. A nice safe and dark place not to be seen dating Bony Bonnie. I was so happy. I had the biggest crush on Tim, but I knew that was a lost cause even if you weren't in the picture, so I went to the drive-in movie. I was afraid. I had never been kissed before. I let the boy do anything he wanted out of fear that if I didn't I would never be asked out again. By morning bell everyone in Rivers Bend High knew I go all the way on a first date."

Bonnie puffed and made sport of her memory. "Shows you how much the class knew. I would have gone all the way before the first kiss! For a good while after that, I used my backside to get the boys to fall over me. I handled the whispering truth about my promiscuity by acting the same way a boy handles his sexuality. Didn't care, and joked about it myself. But it was an act and I did care and hurt when I was joked about."

Sarah picked up her cup. "I didn't visit you to upset you with unpleasant memories." She sipped her coffee and placed the cup back on the table. "I came," she paused. "I would like to be your friend. I'm lonely. I have a great family. John and Lynn. But I really don't have anyone I can call a close friend. I thought of you because I always liked you and because..." she paused.

Bonnie finished speaking for her. "Because of Tim."

Sarah nodded. "Would you mind if I visit you once in a while?"

Bonnie smiled. "How nice. Come anytime, but call first. I'm a single person. So tell me, Sarah, besides not having a close friend, why are you looking so sad? It's your marriage, isn't it?"

"No," Sarah blurted out quickly.

"Sarah," Bonnie smiled. "If we are going to be close friends, speaking to each other openly is the first step."

Sarah lowered her eyes and face. "I made another mistake. But this time I'm sticking it out. That is why I admire you, Bonnie. You seemed to have always worked through your troubles, high school, men," Sarah smiled. "Tim."

Bonnie crushed out her smoking cigarette. "Don't believe it! Now unleash your anguish, best friend!"

Over coffee Sarah told Bonnie how she had come to marry John. "I was lonely. John was lonely. Lonely hearts keep each other company. At first he was against marrying me because of his condition. His wounds from Vietnam are appalling. He's still full of shrapnel. He told me then that the medical experts gave him no promises that he would remain sexually active because the shrapnel inside of him will probably move about as he aged. Any further attempts to remove the shards of metal could be fatal to his sex life or our sex life if we stayed together. During sex, he started having terrible pain and I urged him to take a chance with an operation. Now after several operations, he's living with a urostomy and only scar tissue where testicles had been. So, before I married him I knew the score going in and I was the one that convinced the gentle giant that outside of him, I was no longer interested in the troubles that came with sex and men. Finally, he consented, after also thinking about Lynn and being aware that he could provide her with a swell future. He left me the option to leave the marriage at anytime without explanation."

Bonnie reached across the table and took Sarah's hand. "I didn't know."

"Only a few people do. Family. So, please don't repeat it. Especially to Tim. I don't want him to think I'm some sort of martyr."

"Martyr? Damn, Sarah, what you did, well," Bonnie gasped. "To me, you're as befuddling as Joan of Arc. You don't hear voices too, do you?"

Sarah gave a sad smile. A single tear ran down her cheek.

Bonnie squeezed her hand. "When Tim left me, Sarah, I forced myself to go to work each day when I really felt like cutting my wrist. I can honestly say I got through Tim's rejection of me easier because of my career, but it was hard nonetheless."

Sarah's eyes were wet. "That's why I think of you, Bonnie. You're independent in every way."

Bonnie chuckled. "What other choice did I have? Live with my parents?"

"Do you hear from Tim?" Sarah asked softly.

Bonnie lit another cigarette. "Yes, we write long letters to each other, his is boring stuff."

"He's happy then?" Sarah perked up.

Bonnie blew smoke at her coffee cup. "He'll never be happy. Do you want his address?"

"No!" Sarah jumped in her seat. "I wouldn't know how to begin. What to say to him."

Bonnie laughed hard. "Tell him you love him. I do all of the time." Bonnie let go of Sarah's hand and put in under her chin and lifted her face. "You still do, too, don't you, Sarah?"

"Yes." Sarah murmured and started to cry. "Does John know?"

Sarah wiped her tears away. "I think so, but he'd never ask a question like that. John is wonderful to me and Lynn, and I know this sounds crazy, but I love John, too. He's very special to me and Lynn."

"Ohhh, Sarah!" Bonnie shuddered. "I can't believe what I'm hearing. You sound just like Tim talking about me! Tim loved you, but at the same time he would swear that he loved me too."

"I'm sorry, Bonnie. I didn't mean to open a wound. Tim is better off where he is. He's different."

Bonnie poured them each more coffee, lit another cigarette, unaware that she had one burning in the ashtray. She was feeling happy over Sarah's visit.

"Different?" Bonnie snapped before sitting back down. "Tim is different in only one way. He's full of guilt like you. He wants the world to be a better place. Who doesn't? He wanted to be happy at his work. Who doesn't? He's full of male sexuality, we both know that. His difference is guilt. He wants to personally find God and lay his own guilt at the Almighty's feet. He doesn't want to wait in line at the pearly gates with the rest of us!"

Sarah fiddled with her hands. "Maybe I'll write to him someday."

"What do you think made you fall for Tim? Twice fall for him?" Bonnie asked.

Sarah sighed. "I would say that he made me think. Stirred up my mind about family, culture, even the church." Sarah raised her head up and a sense of pride showed on her face. "Tim will attack the church if he believes it's wrong about something. He doesn't hide his feelings." Then she lowered her eyes again. "He made a new woman out of me, at least mentally, but physically, I lead a life not that much different than my Mom did, or my sisters do."

Sarah looked Bonnie in the eyes. "I think Tim wanted me to be like you, Bonnie. Smart with music and art. But too much had already happened, most of it caused by me, for us to make it together for life. But Tim's time with me won't be wasted. Lynn is being brought up to be more like a Bonnie than a Sarah."

Bonnie lit another cigarette, the two big butts in the ashtray having burned out. "You go to church a lot, don't you, Sarah?"

Sarah nodded. "I feel free in church, in the beauty and serenity surrounding me. Tim would always say that the Catholic Church is the church of the artist."

The two reached across the table and took each other's hands into their own. Bonnie spoke. "Sarah, you have to do what works for you. There is nothing else you can do. Our past is in God's hands to judge, the future in our own. If going to church helps you, go more often. Get more involved, wash down the entire nave. Do whatever it takes to keep happy with yourself. Don't do it as a penance of some sort, but for yourself."

They were smiling at each other. Bonnie spoke. "Do you know what I loved about Tim?"

Sarah shook her head and murmured, "No."

"He made me feel special. Every morning I'd wake up in his arms." Sarah stifled.

Bonnie continued. "Everyday he'd seduce my mind. Sometimes he's just sit around in a fog, thinking of God-knows-what. It drove me crazy. But you're right, Sarah, he is different. In his fog, he wasn't thinking about sports, or cars, or even sex like most men. He was thinking about the missing pieces to God's puzzle and how to put the Garden of Eden...Paradise, back together again." Bonnie let go of Sarah's hands and wrapped her housecoat tight across her breasts. "The next time he comes home, I'll pester the hell outta him to visit you and John."

"Please don't." Sarah giggled. "I'd die if I answered the door and he was standing there."

"Well," Bonnie chuckled. "His ordained butt is definitely going to the garage to see John."

The people moving along the communion line brought Bonnie out of her daydreams. Tim was giving communion to Lynn, placing the host into her cupped palm.

Orson was not in the communion line, but to Tim's fury, he caught him gaping at Lynn on her return to her pew. Fitch was right, Orson was going to try and romance Sarah's daughter.

After communion, Tim returned to the altar for the concluding rite. Brogan took a long look out over the pews of Saint James. John and Sarah had many friends at the end of their lives and Father Tim was glad.

"The Mass is ended, go in peace..."

Tim refused Mr. Reilly's offer, deciding to drive himself to the cemetery. If the snow on the hillside where his parents were buried wasn't too deep, he wanted to make a quick visit to their graves after the graveside services for Sarah and John were finished.

Before the line of automobiles began moving, Tim located the tape he desired on the back seat of his little car. Music for his trip to the graveyard...Richard Strauss' *Death and Transfiguration*.

The music gave Tim the mood of death, a heavy feeling of gloom. Tim knew the music, knew that after a while the sound would transfigure to triumphant beauty. Sarah's body was released from the world, her soul free from death.

The cars began moving. Tim was driving behind Sarah's hearse. He listened to the gloomy music, was being overwhelmed by the meaning, and thoughts of Sarah.

The hearse entered the arched metal gate of Saint James hilltop cemetery. The line of cars wound around the small road until they reached their destination.

While the undertaker directed the movements of the pallbearers, Father Brogan waited by the open graves. He would say a few prayers for the dead and it would be over. He was cold, wearing only a cassock and surplice. He peered into Sarah's open abyss. Who would have thought it would end like this when he walked her hand-in-hand through the parks and streets of Rivers Bend?

The pallbearers struggled with their effort, walking over the snow-covered grounds, taking small and deliberate steps. They reached the graves and placed the caskets on the mechanical devices framing the dark holes. The mourners huddled against one another, insulating each other from the cold currents, wind laced with icy snow. Orson huddled close to Lynn.

Tim raised his hand sluggishly, making the sign of the cross He started his prayers for the dead by shouting into the wind. The people responded when appropriate, chants departed their mouths in vapors, the warm air from their lungs collided with the February cold. Misty prayers blew away from the open graves and mingled with dancing snowflakes.

Tim concluded the prayers. Everyone went carefully to their warm engine running parked cars.

Lynn took Tim by the arm and moved in close to him. She stretched her neck to speak close into his ear. "I have a gift for you. Can you come to the new home tomorrow? I'm packing Mom and Dad's personal things and I'll have your gift there. I want to finish the packing tomorrow."

Tim put his arm around her and smiled down into her face, "I'll be there."

"Good." she said and turned away from him.

Tim watched her walk to the chauffeured limousine. He would have lingered a few more moments by Sarah's grave, but when he realized that the grave diggers were waiting impatiently for him to leave before lowering the coffins, he walked away from Sarah's grave.

Tim stumbled and slid down the snowy hillside, balancing himself on grave stones along the way to his parents graves. Passing his car, he did not notice Bonnie sitting in the passenger seat. He had left the engine running, heater on, and the somber music of Richard Strauss still playing.

When Bonnie saw Tim walk across the road and go further down the hillside, she knew he'd be gone for a while and pushed the eject button, abruptly stopping the music.

"How dreadful!" she moaned and lowered the hood of her coat.

Bonnie looked around the car, picked up a few of the many cassettes littering the seats and floor of the vehicle, and searched for music more to her taste. Before she found anything, Tim returned.

"Surprise!" Bonnie barked as Tim opened the car door.

"Brrrr, quite a surprise."

"Mind if I hitch a ride?"

Tim stared at her. "You cut your hair!" Bonnie's hair was shoulder length and laced with gray strands.

Bonnie laughed. "The correct response, Tim, is, 'I like your hair short, Bonnie.'"

Tim drove slowly away. He looked back at the gravesite. Sarah and John had been lowered into their eternal holes.

Bonnie looked away from Tim and spoke. "When are you leaving?"

"I'm not certain. Do you have a cigarette, Bonnie?"

"I quit. How are you holding up?"

"I'm okay, thanks for asking."

Bonnie cracked the window. "It stinks in here. It needs a good cleaning."

Tim grimaced. "I know."

Tim reached the cemetery gate, drove under its arch and onto the wet city street. He pulled off to the side of the road. "Bonnie," he sighed, and looked straight ahead through the wet windshield and asked, "Would you like to go out to dinner? Tomorrow evening about seven?"

Bonnie looked straight ahead too. A devilish grin spread across her face. "Are your intentions dishonorable?"

Tim chuckled.

CHAPTER SEVENTEEN

Ben turned his head on the big white pillow and blinked a few times at the digital clock. Eight-thirty. In the past, he would've been at the Piano Bar serving his customers by this time. In those days of full employment at the mill, some steelworkers enjoyed a drink before going to the furnace, and the men getting off of the graveyard shift were always reliable customers. Now with only skeleton shifts working at the mill, Ben didn't bother opening the bar until noon or later.

Nothing seemed to be going well for him. The bar was hardly profitable anymore. He no longer had a piano player, his car was broken down, and he was short of cash to have it fixed. He pushed his big overweight frame up and sat on the edge of his king-sized bed. Time to take a shower, time to get dressed, time for work. Dull time alone to be used up in life searching for a life. He stood up. He was naked. He walked to the framed poem hanging on the bedroom wall. The only scrap of anything that he still had from his life before coming to Rivers Bend. He read the poem as he did quite often.

If there were peace in the world,
People would love in a very special way.
People would be kind to each other,
And obey their Father and Mother.
And we should not fight,
Because it is what's right,
And maybe we just might,
Shine like a light.
-Benjamin, Fifth Grade

He'd won a prize for that poem, a blue wooden yo-yo, and it was the only recognition in his dull life he'd ever received. His teacher had the poem framed and his Dad hung it on his bedroom wall. Many hours he spent alone in his bedroom playing with his yo-yo, and he soon became so good at yo-yoing tricks that no other fifth graders in the school yard could match his talent. And all with only one good hand. He was so proud of himself back then.

After shaving, he turned on the shower and carefully maneuvered his fat into the spray. With his good arm, he scrubbed himself, rubbing the bar of soap briskly, watching the suds run down his fair skin.

John and Sarah never came to the Piano Bar, so he felt under no obligation to attend their funerals. However, if he had known Tim was in town he would've gone to the cemetery services yesterday morning just to see him. He liked Tim. He cherished the times they worked together at the Piano Bar. He liked sharing his intellectual side with Tim and found most of his other customers dull to his thoughts.

He felt it was his fault that Tim quit working for him. If he hadn't been so damn lonely, perhaps he would've been more upbeat and not as moody at that time of his life. Just like that...he quit. Said he needed a change. Some change...becoming a missionary priest.

Through all the passing years since Brogan quit the piano bar he could still recall what a huff he had gotten himself into over that lady from Erie. And for what? He never had a chance to get her into his bed. She was too pretty for a misshaped bartender. She was just being friendly and the smiles she gave him that long ago night meant nothing more than what they were meant to be; friendly smiles without an amorous link. Only a withered man with a love-starved imagination would attach wild romantic hopes to polite smiling lipstick covered lips.

He put his balding head under the hot spray. Soon it would be his birthday. Start another year of life alone. At only forty-four, he was already tired of life as he had lived it. Soon after he won the blue yo-yo, his parents were killed in an automobile accident and he was sent off to live with his childless uncle and aunt. His mother's sister was like a Mom to him but his uncle was a bit nasty toward him from time to time, calling him Master Undersized when irritated.

He worked at his uncles' tavern after school; cleaning, washing glasses, and cooking fast foods. His loving aunt died soon after he graduated from high school and when he turned twenty-one, he left the little Northern Pennsylvania town and ventured out on his own. He had few clothes, an old car, but plenty of money from a trust fund his aunt had established for him from his parent's insurance policies.

On his trip south and away from his unkind uncle, he stopped at a motel nearby and noticed a piano bar for sale in a Pittsburgh newspaper. He thought of the possibilities with a steel mill close by. He bought the bar and started a new life.

He promised himself prosperity. He would eat and drink well, dress impeccably, study what interested him, and be a refined gentleman and tavern owner. And if he could get over his fear of women, fear of their rejection, perhaps he would someday receive a go-ahead from a lady and who knows... even marry.

For a while, he accomplished most of what he had promised himself, but he never found a bride. His troubles with women began with high school whispers and giggles about his smaller hand and arm. He retreated further away from his classmates with each passing year of school, and before graduation he begged his aunt to allow him to quit school. But she wouldn't hear of it and he went on and graduated with lower grades than he should have earned.

His new life turned out to be as lonely as his old life. He wanted something to happen in his life, something more than the daily humdrum existence that he endured. He wanted someone to care about and someone to care about him. He turned off the shower and stood there dripping for a while.

He secretly liked Bonnie years ago but she was Tim's woman then and he never let on to her or anyone else how he felt about her. She seldom came to the Piano Bar after Brogan went into the seminary. When she did patronize on occasion over the last twenty or so years, she usually had a male friend to keep her company, a male that didn't have a shrunken hand or other shrunken parts hanging from his body. And besides that, he was terrified by a spunky woman like Bonnie. He had seen her recently and thought she was aging well and in some ways looked prettier now than when she was younger.

He reached for his large-sized bath towel. He felt better after the hot shower. He waxed his mustache and brushed his teeth. The rest of him looked like hell but his teeth still shined with glittering white health. He gave himself a big smile in the mirror. Tim was always good company. Maybe he would stop by Saint James rectory and see if his old piano man was still in town.

He dressed in his charcoal suit, snapped on a red bow tie, and sat on the edge of his bed, struggling over his lump of a belly to get a pair of heavy socks and boots on his feet. He struggled into his overcoat, put a glove on his normal hand, and let his smaller arm and hand hide and dangle inside of the overcoat sleeve. He left his apartment on a hill, cautiously walking down the sidewalk toward the river.

He could see Saint James belfry against the gray winter sky. Cold wind hit his face turning his nose bright red and freezing the waxed tips of his mustache. The sidewalks were clear of snow and ice. Ben was grateful to the row house tenants for clearing the sidewalks and salting the ice in front of their homes.

Midway down the hilly road, he could see the entire gray stone church. He could see the big red doors of Saint James, the stained glass windows, and the red brick rectory with its high pitched roof where he supposed Tim would be staying.

He crossed over River Avenue and headed towards the bridge and the Piano Bar. He went a few steps and then, on impulse turned and began walking through the deep snow covered city park on a straight path to the red doors of Saint James. When he reached the rectory he was breathing hard and reached out and took hold of a statue of Saint James. The stone image was ice cold and the chill quickly found its way through his glove. His bare diminished hand hidden up the overcoat sleeve was getting numb.

After ten minutes, he caught his breath and stepped across the rectory's porch and rang the doorbell. He was having second thoughts and began to turn away when Father Eugene opened the door. He fumbled for the words.

"Is Tim...Ahh. Father Brogan here?"

Father Eugene chuckled. "Not here. He went to see a young lady, a naval officer." Father chuckled again. "Women naval officers, who would have thought?"

"Just tell him a friend stopped by. Thank you. Goodbye."

"I will, if I don't forget. Forget a lot lately."

The old priest forgot to ask him his name and he was glad now to get away from the rectory without revealing who he was. Why talk with a man he hadn't seen in twenty-some years, as if that could cure his loneliness? He headed to the bridge thinking he was losing his mind.

He made it to the bridge but was breathing hard, exhaling frosty puff like a steam train traveling across an open prairie. The Ohio was flowing fast; the currents looked evil and dangerous as if they could swallow a person quickly. It was not the first time he looked down on the river with dark thoughts and visualized the currents taking him away from his lonesomeness.

He pushed on, made it to the other side of the bridge and walking along the side of the road. He had a hired bartender, a family man, and he didn't have the heart to let him go. Often the relief bartender's paycheck was more than he had for himself after paying the bills. The hired bartender started at six this day so he could challenge the bridge once again on his walk home. If he succeeded crossing the span and not taking a final baptism, perhaps he would go to Saint James and visit Tim.

CHAPTER EIGHTEEN

Tim unbuttoned his black trench coat and followed Lynn into the spacious living room while apologizing. "I'm sorry. I meant to get here earlier, but I was just exhausted and slept later than I usually do."

Lynn smiled and waved her hand at him. "You're forgiven, padre."

The house smelled of fresh paint and new carpets. Lynn glanced at Tim. "I have coffee brewing. I hope you like it black. No cream or milk in the house."

"Black will be fine."

"Take off your coat and have a seat while I get our coffee." Lynn walked away. He watched her go to the kitchen with an energetic walk wearing red corduroy slacks and a white sweatshirt. She wasn't wearing any makeup and had her hair bunched on top of her head. He took his coat off and laid it across the back of a sturdy oak chair. Lynn was back with a steaming pot of coffee and two large mugs. Tim stood next to her and watched.

She finished pouring and placed the pot on a potholder in the center of the large teakwood coffee table. She frowned at Tim, "Father Brogan, do you ever wear enough clothes?"

"Tim, please, Lynn."

"At the cemetery you looked half frozen, and now, only a white shirt under that not too heavy coat. You're going to get sick."

"I packed in a rush and brought few clothes with me."

"Please," Lynn opened her arm towards the long new sofa. "Sit, Tim."

They sat close to each other. Neither leaning back into the soft sofa, but both bent at the waist towards the coffee table. "Excuse the way I look," Lynn said touching her hair and placing one hand on his shoulder. "I've been packing things up. The house has a buyer already. An old friend of my parents, Dutch. Do you know him?"

Tim smiled. "Very well."

"My uncle is handling the arrangements for me, but Dutch is taking it all, the house, the garage, everything, even the furniture. I'm only packing up personal things to store away until I get more of a settled life myself."

"So, you don't have much more to do?" Tim asked, taking the hot mug into his hands.

94

"No. Orson has been a big help. He retired early from the mill, and as he said, lives alone with not much to do to keep him busy. And he has a pick up truck. He's already packed up a lot of stuff while I was busy at the funeral home, Dad's old albums, Marine Corps uniforms, and things like that." Lynn took her mug of coffee and held it with both hands, blowing lightly into the brew to cool it down. "He's coming later to help me finish up. I'm expecting him at anytime." She sipped.

The hot mug in Tim's hand sent heat to his cold fingers. He nodded. "I see." Brogan sipped his coffee. She was still talking to him.

"...And that is why I wanted you to stop by. Mom told me that should she die before you, I should see to it that you get this." Lynn reached down onto the sofa beside herself and extended her closed hand. "Mom wanted you to have this." Lynn opened her hand. "She said it was a gift from you."

Tim sat his mug on the coffee table and took the bloodstone rosary from Lynn's hand. He stared at it in the cup of his hand. He had purchased the rosary in El Salvador, deliberately choosing the color red, the color of the heart, the color of love. Lynn was talking.

"Before they closed Mom's coffin, I took the rosary."

Brogan fingered the silver crucifix and put the rosary in his shirt pocket, near to his heart. "I'll cherish it always, Lynn. Thank you."

Lynn started to cry. It was the first breaking emotion she allowed anyone to witness. She turned from Tim, rubbing her eyes. "Excuse me."

"I loved them both, too." Tim muttered.

After a few moments, Lynn regained control of her emotions and thoughts. Took his hand in hers, "I know you did and they loved you too."

They both sipped coffee quietly for some moments. Tim changed the subject. "What about you, Lynn. When are you returning to…ahhh, where are you stationed?"

"Panama. In three days."

"What do you do in the Navy?"

"Intelligence," she answered, appearing in control of herself with only her eyes still glassy.

"Intelligence Officer?" Tim asked, now much more interested in her assignment with the Navy.

Lynn forced a smile at him, nodding her head up and down, strands of her hair falling over her face. "And I'm well aware of the missionary activity in Central America and of the political involvement by many Catholic priests. I don't agree with them, the priests, but I also know that the church most often has better intelligence of the volatile situations in the area than we do at Intelligence." She pinned her hair back up.

Tim held Lynn's hand with both of his and looked into her green tired eyes. "I served in that region for many years. I know it well, and I am not in sympathy with many of the policies our American government has towards those small countries." Tim paused, and then added. "But I don't agree with the leftists either, those that believe only through violence will change come about."

Lynn became alert. "Tim, many priests outright support the guerrillas, you must know that."

"I do. Many priests have given up on reform by peaceful methods, our government." Tim stopped, switched his thoughts. "Well Lynn, this isn't the time for such a discussion." They were still looking into each other's eyes.

"But it is for me, Tim. I need my work to get through this sudden tragedy…"

While Lynn was speaking, Tim studied her facial features searching for Sarah. She was pretty, but without the striking beauty of her mother. She was cute, athletic looking. The only features Tim could recognize that came from Sarah were her eyes and lips. Her full lips were cookie cutter replicas of Sarah's lips. Lips he used to nibble at, lips he ran his finger over, lips that smothered him with affection. Oh, what a puff of pride he was to walk away from their caress.

Lynn was still talking about her work as an Intelligence Officer.

"…I know our own government doesn't put enough pressure on the dictators as long as they keep the leftists subdued…"

Tim had to get his mind into the conversation and off of Lynn's mouth so he added to her sentence. "And bananas are shipped to America cheap." He uttered.

Lynn smiled. "I never thought of that, but you are probably right. Can you give me more of your thoughts about the region?"

"I have many thoughts, Lynn. It's a feudal system, with landowners and dictators controlling the masses instead of kings and princes. America has only urged weak political reform, and much too often empower the military dictators with military equipment and intelligence to surpass their own people." Tim paused, picked up his cooling coffee and looked at Lynn. She seemed interested, her mind away from her sorrow, so he continued.

"Who are these guerrillas? Most are peasants, sons and daughters of peasants that have been convinced by history that change will come no other way except by the gun. Most of those fighters aren't leftist or have any political view. They have only one view, and that is that nobody's going to help them find justice but themselves." Tim's voice had been rising.

Lynn touched his shoulder. "Tim, I didn't mean to touch on an issue that upsets you. I can understand your view; I have a lot of compassion for the peasants and their daily struggle and their small hope. I see the immense wealth of the powerful landlords. I understand, but some in the Navy don't, and cannot understand why priests are in the hills with men of violence."

Tim sighed, controlling his tone. "Those peasants should have the benefit of the sacraments wherever they are, and they certainly have as much right to communion as the powerful and wealthy. Priests must be where they are needed, regardless of political philosophy. It's not the first time priests have been on both sides of the firing line, and it won't be the last."

Lynn refilled their mugs. "The church's record below the border isn't so good either, Tim."

Tim shook his head. "The church made mistakes for centuries in that area. While the European church evolved away from the position of the divine right of kings to rule, the Latin Church seemed stuck in history. Instead of fulfilling its true mission of service to the rich and poor alike, the Latin hierarchy pandered to the wealthy and kept as much power as any middle age bishop."

Lynn sat listening. Both drank from their cups. Tim continued with the feeling that it was good therapy for Lynn.

"The priests living with the peasants kept the true faith, serving the poor, living as they do. The mass of people remained loyal to the church because of humble priests who often suffered as much as they did, but the hierarchy has now changed and no longer is being hand picked by clerical loyalist of the rich families."

Lynn sat her cup down on the table. "I've heard about that. I've been told it's heavy on Marxist thought."

"Why?" Tim smiled. "Because it wants to break up a feudal system. Because it tells the peasants they have dignity, which they deserve, to be treated better and given better wages for their labor? Liberation Theology is no more than a sharp look at how people live, and then reflection on that reality in the face of scripture."

"Will you be going back below the border anytime soon?" Lynn asked.

"No, however, there is a plan that I've been involved with. It's called the American Plan. Have you heard of it?"

Lynn shook her head. "No." then chuckled. "You must remember, Tim. I'm a junior officer. Most of my intelligence work is no higher than drug dealers."

Tim took a big sip of his warm coffee. "Well, it's being kicked around in Washington, probably won't go anywhere. But if it does, I've been asked to go to Central America to study the support for the plan amongst the peasants at the Mesa Grande refugee camp in Honduras."

Lynn's eyes flashed. "Who asked you? Our government?"

"No, no, my superiors asked me because of my long service at missions in Honduras and El Salvador. I know a lot of campesinos. My superiors believe it's a fair plan. It also involves the Japanese, making jobs and giving people a shot at a better life. We'll see what happens, but if I do go to a mission in Central America, I hope we can get to see one another."

Lynn touched his arm. "We must. And Tim...ahh," she took both of his hands into hers. "Do you know what happened? I didn't see you at the funeral home to talk to you about it."

"Only that they both died together, in bed, from a natural gas leak."

Lynn's eyes began watering up. "That's right, Tim." Instead of turning away from him, she fell into his arms, crying against his shoulder. "I'm living a nightmare." she sobbed.

Tim cradled her tight, kissing the top of her head. After she cried herself out, she pulled away from him, took a tissue from the coffee table and wiped her face.

"They had been in the house only three days. A temporary gas line was hit by a truck bringing gravel for the driveway. The landscaping, as you could see when you came, is far from being completed. The blow didn't break the pipe at the place of impact, but caused a weak fracture farther up the line that only started to leak during the night. They died together. An investigation is going on, but that's what happened. Both quietly gassed in Dad's dream house."

Tim remained silent.

"Come with me, Tim." She took him by the hand to a bay window overlooking the backlot of the house to the river's edge. They stood close together peering out the window, holding hands. The many trees between the house and the river had their branches topped with snow.

"Isn't it beautiful? Dad always wanted to build along the river and get Mom out of that old row house by the garage he bought years ago."

"Lynn," Tim paused. "There is something I must talk to you about. Now. About Orson."

Lynn looked up into Tim's face. "What about Orson?"

"He's not the man he is pretending to be. If you are alone with him in this house, you could be in danger."

"What are you saying, Tim? He's my father's cousin. Family. What sort of danger?"

Tim sighed. "Sexual."

"Rape? Orson? Me? Go on!"

Tim pulled her by the hand back to the sofa, sat her down and stood over her. "I'm going to tell you something that happened a long time ago, and well, it also was the beginning of your mother and step father's romance."

Lynn stared up at the tall missionary. Tim told her how Orson had tried to rape Sarah, how Sarah had tricked him, how Orson again went after her with bitterness at the Steak and Ale and how John came to her rescue. When he finished, Lynn just sat with her mouth half open. Then spoke.

"Why didn't someone ever say anything about it? At family functions, Orson was always around."

"I don't know, Lynn. All families put their best face forward."

"Why do you say he might try something with me?"

"Another friend of your father and mother thinks so. Fitch. And I know Orson, he's somewhat sick when it comes to women."

"I'll be damned," Lynn sighed. "And he's been so nice."

"Precisely," Tim muttered. "Nice is not his nature."

"But he'll be coming here soon! Oh, Tim! I don't even want to see him again after what you told me. Trying to rape Mom. Will you help me?"

Tim reached down and took a gulp of his cold coffee. "I have a plan, that is, if you can put off this packing, until tomorrow. Can you?"

"Sure, I'll have a few of my cousins help me."

"Good, then I want you to leave the house now. Lock it up. I'll take care of Orson. Okay?"

Lynn stood and swore. "That bastard!" She ran her hand nervously through her hair. He won't get violent towards you, will he, Tim?"

"No, no, don't worry about that. He just needs to be confronted. Now, come on. Get your coat on and get out of here."

They both put on their coats and stepped outside. Lynn kissed Tim softly on the lips. "Thanks, Tim." She locked the front door.

He smiled. "Don't worry, get going, shoo. I'll be driving behind you for a distance."

Lynn rushed to her car and drove over the gravel driveway and onto the paved wet road towards town. He followed close behind.

Several miles before Rivers Bend at a solitary spot near a railroad crossing, he pulled over to the side of the two-lane road, stopped his car, and waited with his engine idling.

Tim leaned back in the seat, gazing through the windshield, over the hood of the compact car, and beyond the field of snow before the ground fell abruptly to the river.

The Ohio was flowing swiftly. Sheets of ice were sailing in clusters on the water's surface. Tim could see the Rivers Bend Bridge in the hazy distance, the gray winter sky hanging over the town, Rivers Bends dwellings barely traceable in the afternoon mist.

He twisted about in the little seat, reaching for cassettes scattered on the back seat and floor. He found one to soothe his wrathful mood and slid it into the stereo. The Mills Brothers began harmonizing to him.

He glanced down the wet road for a sign that Orson was coming his way. The wet road surface gave off a black mirror reflection that hurt his light blue eyes. The boundary of the road was defined by banks of dirty snow. Everything outside of his warm car appeared lifeless and frozen, even the bird perched on the power line.

He leaned into the windshield and stared at the bird. A pigeon? A crow? A black spot on the wire. The bird seemed undisturbed by the cold wind, the blowing snow, and the icicles hanging under its feet. He turned the car window down to look hard at the bird. It must be dead, frozen in place, dead to the cold, dead to him, only waiting for the sunshine to melt its icy grip and let it tumble to the ground.

He shut the window, thinking about the black dot. Not long ago it was in a nest, full of energy, sharing warmth with its siblings. It was protected and cared for by its mother, and now it was still, cold, clay. The earth would consume it, feathers and all, just as it was consuming Sarah and would eat him, too, someday. Life was too short. He couldn't suppress his loneliness any longer. He made up his mind. He would satisfy his desire. At least he wouldn't be committing adultery with Bonnie.

The Mills Brothers faded. The tape was rewinding when he saw a pick up truck coming. He drove across the road, blocking Orson's way. Orson slammed on the brakes and swerved his truck to avoid hitting Tim's car. The priest got out of his car leaving the car door open. He walked to Orson who was turning down his window.

Orson shouted at him. "Are you nuts? What the hell's a wrong with you?"

Tim bowed down to the open window and Orson's clean-shaven face. A strong smell of lotion hit Tim's nostrils. "Where are you heading, Orson?"

"None of your damn business." Orson began winding up the truck's window.

Tim gripped the top of the upward moving window. "Don't shut me out of your life, Orson, I know too much." Brogan grinned.

Orson looked quizzical at Tim through the half opened window. "You're one crazy priest! Whata you know? Huh? Get your car outta my way."

"Your services aren't needed anymore, Orson. Lynn is gone, the house is locked up."

Orson looked perplexed. "Okay, what's this all about? What's goin'on?"

"It's about a lot of things, Orson. About you trying to rape Sarah. About you..."

Orson cut him off. "Christ. That was long ago! A misunderstanding. I have regrets."

Tim stood straight up, laughing a harsh sound. "Regrets! You bastard! You're on your way now to hit on her daughter smelling like a musk deer!"

Orson protested. "No, I'm not! I'm goin' to help her pack."

"Sure, Orson, in you turtleneck and leather jacket. And God, what is that smell you splashed on yourself? It's no wonder you have to force yourself on women."

Orson stared up at him through the half-open window. "You're full of it."

Tim stepped back from the truck. "I told Lynn everything, how you tried to rape her mother, how John grabbed your nuts. That must've hurt." Tim paused and then lied. "How you screwed over our friend Fitch by sleeping with his wife. I just told her things like that, you know...the truth... and as a wise Teacher said, 'the truth will set you free.' Free enough, Orson, for you to examine your life and overcome what is lurking behind your face. It's time to grow up, pal."

Orson was gripping his steering wheel, his eyes narrowed. "And what's lurking, a pussy fancy? What's wrong with that? We're not all crazy and cloistered like you."

Tim covered his ear. "Ouch! That hurt." Tim pointed his finger at him. "No, friend. With you it's more frenzy then fancy; you're like a blind mole, spending up your life in pursuit of goodies, terrified to stop seeking more and more because then there might be only wholesome things to do. Quit prowling! Kill the mole, read some books, go to a play, take up a hobby, and then you may not have to force your handsome self upon intelligent women." Tim dropped his arm to his side.

"Is the sermon over, Father?" Orson questioned with a straight face. "Can I snuff out the altar candles?"

Tim put his cold hands into his pocket. "As far as you getting to Lynn, I already blew the candles out. I'll move my car. Go to the house and see for yourself. It's locked up. Lynn is gone with a head full of truths about you."

Orson turned his head away and sneered. "I oughta come out there and kick your altar boy ass."

"You probably should. You probably could. But the important thing is Lynn doesn't want to lay eyes on you again. That's worth more to me than a bloody nose."

Orson squinted his eyes. "I'm going up to the house. If she's gone and running around telling all of your bullshit to the women in my family, I'm gonna fix your celibate ass, gonna get you back sooner than you think. I know some shit, too."

"Yeah! Yeah! Yeah! Orson. I'll give you absolution ahead of time." Tim turned and walked away, climbed into his car and backed it up, letting Orson go on his way.

He was ready to drive away when he saw a small branch fall to the ground from an oak tree and was moved by a sentiment. He got back out of the car and walked toward the tree and river, climbing over the dirty snow bank and through the icy dead brown bushes mangled by freezing temperatures. When he got to where the branch had fallen, he picked it up and wrote in the field of snow. "Tim loves Sarah."

He tossed the twig into the river, struggled to his car and drove to Saint James.

CHAPTER NINETEEN

Upon his return to the rectory, Tim found Father Eugene in his favorite spot in the living room, napping on the sofa with the television on. He did not disturb the pastor, but quickly dressed in Father Eugene's cope. He was willing to do as he's always done on his short stays at Saint James; help the old priest tend to his flock.

He left the rectory through the back door and quickly crossed the short distance to the convent. The teaching nuns no longer lived in the building. Now the convent was used by senior citizens and was renamed Saint James Manor.

Inside the hot building, old people sat around the recreation room playing cards, talking and watching television. He sat with some of them, listening to their tales of days gone by and showing interest in what they had to tell him.

After a bit, Tim went to the convent chapel. The small plain wooden altar had candles burning for benediction. Above the altar was a crucifix carved from cherry wood. He had never seen a crucifix so symbolic. Hanging from Jesus' girdle was a handsaw and hammer, a crucified carpenter.

He loved the Catholic way of allowing and encouraging its followers to express their love for God through art and shunning the notion that it's all idols carving idolatry. And what an overflowing treasure of talent the centuries brought forth to the church. Immortals like Michelangelo and Raphael as well as simple folk creations of beauty for gifts to the Heavenly Holy and their local parishes.

He loved the beauty, the pageantry, the expression of love and praise to the Almighty by artful adoration. He could never be anything but Catholic at heart, even now as he planned and hoped to bury his vow of chastity by embracing the forbidden fruit of Bonnie. His heart would still beat Catholic.

The chapel with three rows of dark stained pews was slowly being filled with senior citizens. He studied the aging forms, drained of youth and vitality, only steps from death. Passing time praying to God until their heartbeats faded away and they fell to the ground like the spot on the wire. A spry gentleman assisted him acting as an altar boy. He began the opening song. Many of the elderly sang along.

When benediction was over, he lingered in the chapel praying that the Almighty would forgive him in advance for doing what he believed he had to do to remain sane. In his thoughts, he screamed to God for approval of his pending vow-breaking seduction of Bonnie, using the same reasoning God had used when plucking Adam's rib. 'It's not good for man to be alone.'

He felt someone beside him. "Ben!" he whispered aloud. "What a surprise, Boss!"

Ben unbuttoned his overcoat. "Only have a few minutes, just wanted to stop by and see you."

"I'm glad that you did," Tim chuckled and added, "you still have that esteemed look about you."

Ben reached over and patted Tim on the knee.

"Thanks for the flattering remarks, but I'm a lonely aging fat man. Back when you played for me, I was a lonely flabby young man, which was more of a shame. Young people shouldn't be lonely. I'm sick of being lonely now, and I was sick of being lonely then." Ben gave Tim a great grin. "What's your God going to do about it?"

Tim took Ben by the arm and whispered into his ear. "You mean loneliness for a woman, not in general, don't you, Ben?"

Ben nodded. "You would think I'd get used to it since there never was a woman in my life, my entire existence. Since adolescence I've longed for a girlfriend, a lover, a wife. I feel so unfulfilled, like an empty brontosaur."

Brogan giggled "You, telling me about loneliness?"

A burst of laughter shot from Ben's throat. He covered his mouth with his hand. "Aren't you supposed to be quiet in church?" he mumbled and gained control of his own giggles. "It is funny, why the hell am I coming to you for advice about women? A jungle missionary priest!"

Ben turned and looked at the altar with its candles still burning. "I never belonged to any church, even as a child. As a blooming young adult I was too concerned about gossiping classmates teasing me to dwell on a God."

Tim didn't know what to say after he saw Ben's eyes glistening. Ben was on the verge of breaking down. The pain of rejection over his lifetime was brewing to a head and a force inside the big man was getting out of control.

The first tears rolled down Ben's chubby cheeks and soon he was sobbing. Some old people peeped into the chapel from the adjoining room. Tim shooed them away with a waving arm.

He let Ben sob without comment. When the tears quit coming, Ben took a handkerchief from his pocket and wiped his face, "I'm sorry."

Ben stood up slowly and looked down on his former piano player. "Well, I'll repeat myself. How is your God going to help me out?"

Tim put both hands on his head. "I hope by more means than sending you to me!"

Ben buttoned up his coat. "I should've seen a therapist long ago."

Tim stood. "Ben, a few hints. Lose some weight. Second, every man doesn't meet his mate in a bar. Join a club, an organization, a church. There are women at those places too. Try fishing in different water. And I'll pray that you catch a beauty. A catch you won't have to throw back."

"I'd be thankful." Ben uttered, and then added. "I'd never throw someone back, been thrown back too many times myself."

"And you never drown!" Tim added quickly. "Where there's life, there's hope."

"So true!" Ben said laughing. "Such wisdom I can get from any drunk at the bar!"

Tim shot back. "What are friends for?"

"Perhaps hitching a ride home?" Ben answered quickly.

CHAPTER TWENTY

Bonnie waited inside the vestibule of her apartment building, pressing her small nose against the revolving glass door, peering to the end of the walkway. The walkway was clear of snow and well lit, but she couldn't see any headlights on the road beyond.

She stepped back and saw her reflection in the glass panel. She thought she looked as good as she could make herself look without overdosing on cosmetics. Her face, made up with a wee amount of rouge, looked plain and natural. She moistened her small lips. They were kissable, she thought and applied just a thin smear more of lipstick, then popped a mint into her mouth. She liked her hair short with the streaks of gray. She'd gained a few pounds and to her startled mind, she had been getting compliments from men lately at work and on the street.

She moved around in the vestibule, her long white winter coat fitting her well, forming over her extra pounds into her waist. The hood on her coat, collapsed behind her neck, formed a furry white background, framing her thick, short hair. Under her coat she wore a full tan skirt and pale green blouse with a low neckline. Fur lined brown boots covered her ankles.

She figured Tim would come to her for relief if given the opportunity. That is why she schemed and hitched a ride with Dutch and his wife to the cemetery, then cornered him for a ride back to town. She would use her biting wit to cheer him up. Smash any sad thoughts he held over Sarah's death. She had done it before in the sixties. Bony Bonnie polished him up, nagged him back to life, only to lose him to God.

Headlights flashed outside through the glass doors. She knew that this night out with Tim would be better than the last. Back then after being at odds with each other and fighting over Sarah and raindrops, he crushed any dreams she held about him being with her forever. He told her of his thoughts, his secret plans of entering a seminary and becoming a missionary priest. She wanted to shove him overboard for revealing that horrible news to her while cuddling on a romantic river cruise around Pittsburgh's Golden Triangle.

In her mind, he had decided to love Sarah alone instead of with another woman. When she cried, he said that he held a hidden desire to be a missionary since his Navy days. She never believed him. His tormenting Sarah memories had won him away from her. Memories of Sarah alone are what he desired to live with, alone and undisturbed behind the hallowing symbols of the church.

Bonnie saw a car stop outside. Her heart jumped. She spun the revolving door and ran to Tim smiling broadly at her through the open car window. "Tim!" Bonnie gasped, running around the car and getting in before he finished closing his window.

Big band music came from the stereo. Bonnie recognized Glenn Miller's, *In the Mood.* They hugged in the small front seat for many moments without speaking. His unexpected cheerfulness and long squeeze was a surprise to her, and she began getting her hopes up that perhaps he was in the mood too. He let go of her and they both settled back into the car seats. Bonnie turned Glen Miller way down low.

"Where to?" he asked.

Bonnie joked. "Pittsburgh."

"Pittsburgh it is!" Tim answered, putting the car in gear and driving off.

Bonnie perked up. "Really?"

"Pittsburgh, here we come!"

Bonnie touched his sweater. "Don't you own a coat? It's too cold for just a sweater."

"I'll be fine. It's Irish wool, warmer than it looks."

Something off the car seat fell to the floor. "What the hell am I sitting on?" she laughed.

"Cassettes." he apologized. "Sorry, they're all over the car."

She gathered up a few cassettes nearest her and started reading the titles out loud before pitching them one by one over her shoulder onto the back seat. "Elvis, Kenny Rogers, Beethoven, Dolly Parton, Ray Charles, Nat King Cole, Dorsey, Peggy Lee, Platters, and last but not least, The Mills Brothers. Is this how you spent my money, that cash I sent you for those sad looking children? The ones you kept sending me pictures of when you were in Central America? And no hard rock?"

Tim chuckled. "Not for me. I like music that draws out my emotions," he paused. "Even emotions associated with bad memories. The music I like can chocolate coat bad memories and make my sadness or regret or bitterness digestible. Hard rock draws nothing from me, only infuses me with primitive passion. The differences between music that I like and hard rock are like the difference between the Sistine Chapel and spray paint walls. I don't want music to put feeling into me; I want music to draw feeling out of me."

"Wow!" Bonnie raised her eyebrows. "That was a bit more than I wanted to know."

Brogan laughed. "I miss your wit, Bonnie. God, you bring me back to life."

"Don't mention Him either. I used that extraordinary large Bible you sent me as a doorstop. What a gift. Don't you missionaries have any practical gifts like pots and pans?"

They both started laughing. Bonnie received a surprise. He reached over and took her hand. She said nothing, only slid closer to him, a few cassettes she missed sending to the back seat fell to the floor. They interlocked their fingers. She put his hand into both of hers.

They passed over the Rivers Bend Bridge and soon rode by the Piano Bar. Only two cars were in its parking lot. The building looked dim, few lights were on, the blue and green neon light broken, only partially lit.

"It looks pretty run down." Tim said.

"The whole town is run down." Bonnie answered. "It's terrible around here, the mill is barely producing, so many out of work. The only busy place in Rivers Bend is the food bank."

"It's not going to get any better." Tim sighed. "The days of heavy industry in this part of the country are over."

Bonnie made the next move. She moved one hand and touched the back of his head, playing with his hair. He answered her move in a soft voice. "Your hand feels good. Being close to you feels good. Being with you feels good."

She stroked the back of his head harder. Glenn Miller was rewinding.

The highway ahead had dangerous curves. He let go of her hand and drove with both hands on the steering wheel. When the road straightened out, he again put his hand on her lap. She took it into her free hand and looked at him. He was thinking...in his foggy mind something was bothering him. She brought Sarah's name up. "I'm sorry about Sarah. We became pretty close friends." then she laughed. "After you got out of our lives."

He pulled his hand from hers and grabbed the steering wheel with both hands and turned a hairpin curve onto the entrance ramp to the expressway. He drove under the sign with an arrow pointing the way to Pittsburgh.

"Whew, I forgot about that hairpin." he said and went back to his deep thoughts.

Bonnie took his hand back into hers and held it tight on her lap. *In the Mood* began playing again. Tim didn't seem to mind that she brought up Sarah, but she wasn't certain of his mood. Maybe he wanted to talk about Sarah, even her death. "Tim," she asked, "what are you thinking about?"

"About whether I should ask you something." he smiled.

"What?"

"Did you know about John's condition? That he..."

She stopped him. "For a long time. Sarah told me all about it. I told you, we became good friends."

He glanced at her. "And you never told me?"

"T'was none of your business, Tim." She laid her head on his shoulder and spoke very soft to him. "It really wasn't, Tim."

"You're right...it's not my business, but I can't help but wonder..."

Again she cut him off. "If they ever had sex?"

Tim nodded. "It's terrible of me, I know, but I keep wondering."

Bonnie laughed. "It's called being human. In the beginning of their relationship they did, but after a few years and some operations, John lost that ability...now don't ever ask me anymore about it!"

They drove the dark interstate in silence. She kept stroking the back of his neck. A light snow began to fall. He hunched himself over the steering wheel, peering into the night, the snowflakes dancing in front of the car lights like ghostly insects in a swarm.

She kept rubbing him and wondering if his mood would ruin their night together.

"Tim, what else are you thinking about? Something is bothering you. Tell me."

He stayed bent to the steering wheel watching the wet highway. "Don't worry. It's going to be a good night out for both of us. I'm just a little nervous."

"Nervous?" She pulled away from his shoulder and stared at him. "Now what in this world would make Tim Brogan nervous?"

He smiled. "You'll just have to wait and see, or hear, or something."

He slowed the car down and took the exit ramp. He stopped at a red light. They looked into each other's eyes. He kissed Bonnie softly on the lips.

The light turned green. He spoke while driving. "We'll take the incline up to Mount Washington, eat a candlelight dinner, I made reservations, and well...we'll go from there."

She fell back into her seat in mild shock and sighed. "Made reservations? Coming to Pittsburgh for dinner was planned? You knew I'd ask to go to Pittsburgh?"

He drove towards the incline station. "I took a guess that you would."

She collapsed in her seat murmuring. "You know me too well. I haven't had one in years, but now I could go for cigarette."

Tim agreed. "Me too."

They were the only passengers on the red cable car as it lifted up over the steep hillside of Mount Washington. Bonnie held Tim tight around the waist watching the expanding panoramic view of the Steel City beneath them. The snowfall was light, the night sky was clear. The lights from Pittsburgh's skyscrapers and bridges reflecting on the three rivers below mixed with their emotions and overwhelmed them. It was beautiful and he kissed her again, this time very fervently and long. He whispered to her. "You're breathtaking, Bonnie."

She was too full of joy to say or do anything other than to hold him in a bear hug grip around his waist until they reached the top of the mount. They left the incline station and walked around aimlessly, hand in hand, kissing now and then, and killing time until it was time for their dinner.

Inside the Tin Angel Restaurant, Bonnie checked her coat and a tall hostess guided them through a shadowy dining area. The table tops gave off a flickering glow from the candle lights and the well-dressed diners appeared as silhouettes.

Through the restaurant's glass panes, Pittsburgh's bright lights and rivers were showcased as if the diners were viewing the city nestled inside a high and cozy bird's nest. They were seated at a small table. He ordered Chardonnay. The waitress lit the candle on their table and departed. She leaned to Tim. "I need a cigarette."

He walked to the bar and returned to a tense Bonnie with a pack. She lit one up and laid the pack on the table. Out of the dark, the waitress brought their wine, filled their glasses, and moved off into shadows.

Bonnie's eyes were smiling. She leaned to Tim and whispered. "Why did you have to become a priest?"

He whispered back. "The answer is because I like being a priest. The question should be why am I not allowed to marry?"

She grinned. "I'm glad you're not allowed. Shit, then I'd lose even this little bit of you to a wife."

He sipped his wine and gazed down on the rivers, the Gateway Clipper was sailing the Allegheny. He did not look at her while he spoke. "Bonnie, I asked you to dinner tonight for a very special reason." He turned and smiled at her.

She put out her cigarette, looking perplexed.

"I'm making a career move."

She picked up her wine glass, tilted it, swirled the wine and looked at him with widening eyes. "What are you saying?"

He blurted it out. "I'm leaving the priesthood."

Her small eyes got wider. "When?"

"By fall, no later than Thanksgiving. I'd leave sooner but I committed myself to a project in Central America over the summer. If, and I repeat if, a certain American Plan is agreed upon between our government, the governments of Central America and Japan. If no agreement is reached by June, I'll quit before July Fourth.

The waitress came for their order. Both ordered steak. Well done.

Over dinner, Tim explained in detail the American Plan for the economic assistance to the small countries of Central America. After they finished their meals and had their tabled cleared, they both lit a cigarette. It tasted good to Brogan.

"What are your plans after you quit? What are you going to do?"

His eyes were sparkling. "Get married!" He waited, enjoying the paralyzed look on her face. "That is why I asked you to dinner tonight."

She drew back from him. Tossed her cigarette in the ashtray.

"Will you marry me, Bonnie? Sometime later this year?"

She couldn't answer him, only gaped.

"I love you, Bonnie, I do. I loved Sarah, too. I gave up Sarah out of male stupidity. I gave up you for a young man's dream, a vision to make the world a better place. Sarah is dead and the world is still a mess. I don't want to give up any more of me. I cannot live without a woman any longer. I want that woman to be you." He put his cigarette out and took her hand. "I'll come home to you as much as possible until, and if, I leave for Central America. Or we can meet halfway, some little town close to the New York border if you're up to driving a hundred miles for a secret rendezvous."

Bonnie drank all of her wine at once and motioned with her glass for Tim to refill it. He did, and his own. "Bonnie," he whispered loud. "Will you answer me? Will you marry me?"

"Yes, yes, yes, I'll marry you!" she started to cry.

He reached over and touched her cheek. Rubbing it gently with the back of his long fingers. "After a few more glasses of wine," he paused, "I want to spend this night with a naked Bonnie in my arms." Then he gave her a devilish grin. "What are my chances?"

She wiped her eyes. Tried to joke. "Well, now, I'll have to think about it. My apartment or the rectory?"

He smiled. "I was thinking more on the lines of the Pittsburgh Hilton."

"The evening gets better and better." she said and lit another cigarette. "I feel like Cinderella." then quipped. "Did she smoke?"

He lit up also.

She took a deep puff and showed concern in her face. "Tim, darling, I love you, but I don't want you as my husband if you're going to be full of guilt because you broke your priestly vow."

He got serious and fiddled with his burning cigarette. "It's clear in my mind that Jesus did not care if those who follow in the apostle's shoes are married or not. The vow I took was a condition established by the church, not Christ. A vow I wouldn't have had to make if Christ were on earth today. Therefore, I'm disavowing it. The church will sooner or later see the folly of a mandatory celibate priesthood in modern times. There is no good reason for the practice to continue. As far as sex is concerned, the Bible speaks out against sexual perversion," he fingered his cigarette. "Rather harshly, I'd say, toasting the citizens of Sodom and Gomorrah was a strong statement on that subject. But sex between single people in love, well, Jesus never said a thing about sex, except for condemning adultery. I think Christ understood that adults in love would have a strong urge to express it to each other." He lowered his eyes from hers and put his cigarette in the ashtray. "You still haven't answered me. Will you love me tonight?"

She grinned. "I can't wait to tarnish your halo!"

They finished their wine, decided against drinking more, left the restaurant and rushed to the cable car. The little red car was waiting and again they were its only riders. As the car descended its track, down the hillside, down to the bustling city, down to the Hilton, he kissed her on the nose. "There is one thing I forgot to mention. Ahh, I don't have enough money left for a hotel room." he grinned into her shining brown eyes. "Do you have any money... on you?"

She squeezed him. "Enough to stay the weekend!" Then she nibbled at his ear and whispered, "That is if you're man enough to last a weekend."

He patted her behind. "We'll see."

CHAPTER TWENTY ONE

In mid-afternoon, Father Eugene was taking his nap and sound asleep on the living room sofa. Tim had said farewell to him earlier that morning when returning to the rectory after spending another wonderful night sleeping with Bonnie. Now it was time to go back to New York. He already packed his car and only needed to telephone Bonnie before driving away.

Bonnie had agreed to drive to Erie every Friday, about the halfway point to the seminary. They would meet in Erie, spend the weekend together and plan for their future. He dialed her number from the rectory kitchen phone. She took off from work for this farewell message he had promised to make before leaving Rivers Bend. He heard her voice.

"Tim!"

He whispered into the phone. "I love you."

"When are you leaving?"

"Now."

He heard her sigh. "Phone. Call collect every night. Promise."

"I will. And Bonnie, would you do me a favor?"

"Anything."

"Look in on Ben at the Piano Bar once in a while. He's very lonely. He could use some of your funny fire to burn his blues away."

"I'll try, but I won't feel like a spitfire with you in New York."

"Bye," he whispered. "I'll see you Friday. Drive carefully." He could hear her tears falling through the phone. He hung up.

He left the rectory and crossed over the snowy grounds to the church. He went inside and stood in the center of the middle aisle. He lifted his head to the choir loft where as a child he stood at his mother's side. From his organ-playing mother, he got a fondness for music and from her brother, the Choir Master of Saint James, vigorous instruction in Latin and voice training.

He walked down the aisle and sat in the front pew. He would never again say Mass at Saint James. Perhaps never again say a Mass; he hadn't as yet made up his mind to that nagging question. He said a few prayers, stood up, crossed himself, and walked outside, got into his little car and drove away.

Crossing the Rivers Bend Bridge, he slid a cassette into the stereo and let Sinatra sing to him.

CHAPTER TWENTY TWO

Gypsy played with the coins in front of her, pushing them about with her finger on the black bar top. The bar was full of men and smoke. She was the only woman in the corner neighborhood tavern.

She sipped her glass of beer, nursing it, very aware that the change she was playing with was the only money she had to her name. Fitch and drinking money were things she had always taken for granted.

It was dark inside the bar and the men were standing in huddles talking loudly amongst themselves. She sat alone on a high stool at one end of the bar thinking about her marriage. Fitch was nice, but she never loved him. She thought she had some false idea that she would one day grow to love him, but she wasn't sure about that thought. From the start of their courtship she knew she'd be able to run wild on him without penalty. Fitch was nice, but not exciting.

She lit a cigarette and counted those remaining inside the pack. She would need more smokes soon, too. The thought of returning to her empty house without anything to smoke was dreadful and added to her frustrations. She inhaled deeply, holding the smoke inside a short time before allowing it to leave her lungs through her nostrils. She sipped some beer.

The bartender put a full glass of beer in front of her while nodding his head in the direction of the man that bought it for her; a stranger standing alone at the opposite end of the bar. She smiled at the man and beckoned for him to come and sit beside her.

The next day when she awoke, the gentleman had already left her bed and house. It was only a few hours ago that he left her side, but already she couldn't recall if his name was Fred or Ted. His name didn't matter to her, but she did fret over her forgetfulness lately. One thing she was sure of on this late morning weekday was that Orson would be home so she dialed his number. She heard his voice.

"Hello."

"Guess who?" she sang.

Orson hung up.

She poured herself a cup of coffee and sat in her bathrobe at the kitchen table. The kitchen was a mess, smelling of stale everything and not cleaned since Fitch left town. Dirty dishes were scattered about in every location of the room. Unopened mail was piled on the table and towels and clothes hung over chairs. Cigarette butts littered the floor, but she wasn't alarmed by the way her kitchen looked, or over Orson's nastiness. He was a nasty person by nature. She only wanted to be with him and his nastiness.

She swallowed some black coffee and lit a cigarette from one of the several packs Fred or Ted got her as a token of his appreciation for spending the night in her bed. She was happy to have so many cigarettes.

She got up from the table and went to the cabinet above the sink and took out a bottle of cheap whiskey. After several big gulps, she felt better. She switched on the radio atop the refrigerator and tuned into the oldie but goodie station. The smoldering cigarette hanging from the corner of her lips sent swirling smoke into her eyes. She narrowed her eyes. Holding onto the bottle, she started back to the kitchen table but got her feet tangled up in some dirty clothes she had discarded on the floor. Bending over with squinting eyes to untangle herself, she stumbled and fell, hitting her head hard against the edge of the table top. The whiskey spilled on the floor and mixed with her blood as the burning cigarette rolled from her mouth.

CHAPTER TWENTY THREE

A summer thunderstorm passed over Rivers Bend making the early July evening cool. Bonnie had waited until the dark clouds blew east and sunshine pierced the light gray sky before starting her walk to the Piano Bar. She held a letter in her hand.

The downpour cleansed the streets and sidewalks as the water gathered and flowed down the hilly streets, washing the dirt and grime into the city's sewage system.

She walked briskly, wearing white shorts and an orange sleeveless blouse. She was enjoying the fresh clean feeling the aftermath left in the air. Tomorrow was the Fourth of July, but Bonnie had no plans to celebrate. They city of Rivers Bend could not afford a fireworks gala. It had nothing to be rejoicing about and neither did Bonnie.

Tim had left the country and the steel mill had shut down. It's cold furnace sat behind locked gates like an abandoned temple to a lost civilization...a dirty monument to wonder at, a remembrance to the Steel Barons of yesteryears. Once a sign of hope and promise for the faithful to live the good life, the mill now stood as an idol; a false god fallen from grace to the youth of the region. Its grimy structures silhouetted against the stark sky without any hope of resurrection.

She raised the letter, studied the handwriting, touched the written words to her heart. It was not her letter, but her love for the man who wrote it made it loving to her. The letter was for Ben, sent from Honduras and written by Tim. Brogan had enclosed Ben's letter along with his letter to her in the same envelope, and now she walked along River Road on her way to the Piano Bar to give it to the bar owner.

This letter was not the first letter Tim sent to Ben through her. She knew that this clever method was nothing more than his way of ensuring she carried out her pledge to visit the lonely fat man.

An airliner flew overhead sending its whiny noises down upon Rivers Bend, but she didn't look up. It was an aircraft like that which took her beloved Tim far away and left her all alone.

She started walking over the Rivers Bend Bridge. The rushing water, dangerously high from the storm, made her think of Tim's insatiable urges to flow to other people and cultures hoping to find solutions for problems that may never be fixed. When the American Plan was approved by the governments involved, like the gushing waters below, his desperation to get to those foreign shores surged. He was excited over the Plan and the hope for a better existence it would bring to that region of the world. He wrote her that his anxiety over the American Plan was not the Plan itself, but his longing for it to be implemented soon, so that he could start his new life with her. She knew better. He was excited about being part of the Plan.

She picked up her pace while gazing out over the safety rail. They had met in a motel in Erie every weekend from February until he left in June. They dined and walked the beaches of Presque Isle. But the best part of each Erie weekend was in the motel room, holding, kissing, and loving one another. It was at the tip of Presque Isle that he told her that the American Plan had been funded and he would be going to Honduras. He had a bad habit of selecting romantic spots to report sad news, and she had told him so.

She stepped off of the bridge and walked in the dirt alongside the road. An eighteen-wheeler came off the bridge behind her. A flatbed, carrying a piece of equipment, a piece of the steel mill being taken from Rivers Bend. The truck driver toot, toot, toot his horn at her. She smiled to herself, raised her long bare arm and waved without turning around.

She strayed from the side of the road onto a grass field and walked under a row of elm trees that stretched to the paved parking lot of the Piano Bar. Only two cars were in the lot and Ben's wasn't one of them. She guessed his car wasn't running again and was being repaired at Dutch's garage.

Playing mailman for Tim was causing her some concern. She enjoyed the walks to the bar, especially on cool summer evenings, but she was beginning to be troubled about Ben and what she sensed when alone in his company.

Ben seemed to like her as more than a friend. Their conversations were always friendly and polite, yet, beneath his surface, she could detect that he desired more than friendship.

When he was alone with her, he made a deliberate effort to keep his withered arm and hand out of her line of sight, turning his big body in ways that kept his crippled parts hidden from her view. She hoped that she was wrong. She understood rejection, having suffered from it many times herself, and wished not to hurt any man desiring her charms.

Ben was busy behind the bar and didn't see her come in through the open door. He still tried to remain an impeccable dresser, but his expensive clothing, purchased in better times, now began revealing its age and in spots was worn and frayed. His hair kept thinning, enough now to reveal his entire scalp beneath the reddish strands of hair.

A few men stood around the bar, steel workers, all standing alone in private thought. All quiet, smoking and drinking beer. All dressed in working clothes with no place to go. After greeting her, Ben poured her a glass of ginger ale. After handing him his letter, she took the refreshing drink to the Baby Grand and sat on the piano bench. Ben read Brogan's letter.

Mesa Grande
Refugee Camp

Dear Ben,
I was overjoyed to receive your letter but saddened by its contents. Ben, you must work through your pain with a qualified person. Being healed is worth the expense! Your personal experience with depression, hidden anger, loneliness, does give you a special insight into the suffering of others...

Ben was distracted. Out of the corner of his eye, he could see Bonnie perched on the bench, her long bare legs crossed. He willed his mind to Tim's letter.

...perhaps your arm is not the deterrent that you feel keeps you from meeting women and developing an intimate relationship. It could be the anger that you think is well hidden within you. But women, I believe Ben, are much more perceptive than men. They can sense your anger without necessarily knowing what it is or where it came from. Jealousy and anger are very hard to totally conceal...

Ben lifted his eyes to Bonnie standing at the jukebox with her back to him, her slim body tan from summer sun. He lowered his eyes, read on.

Camp news. As I wrote to you before, the camp is administered by the United Nations. The only sin the refugees committed was living in guerilla controlled areas. In El Salvador, they lived in a crossfire of suspicion. The government distrusted them and the guerillas recruited them, demanding provisions from them and expecting their support for the cause. The villages had some people supporting the guerrillas while others backed the government...

The first sounds of Jerry Lee Lewis and *Whole Lotta Shakin' Goin' On* got Bonnie's legs and rump wiggling in place to the beat and sent Ben's eyes to her backside. After a few moments of gawking, he read on.

...there is promising news. Japan is establishing assembly plants that will produce electronic products in several key locations in Central America. The idea is to provide jobs for the campesinos who now can only earn wages by cutting sugar cane or clearing land for the rich. The workers would get fair wages and some benefits...Why Japan? I was told they have a vested interest in Central America being stabilized. It seems that almost half of the commercial ships passing through the Panama Canal fly the Japanese flag. Since all of the guerilla activity in the Central American countries are interwoven and cannot be localized, Panama...

Bonnie quit gyrating just as Ben took another peep at her. She looked cool and refreshed, her sleeveless blouse loose fitting, her shoulder length hair tied up in back with a white cloth band. He tried to read Tim's letter.

...many in Congress believe Japan gets a free ride on its own defense, with Japan being under America's defense umbrella and saving them much yen...

He raised his eyes again to her backside. The music stopped and she abruptly turned around and caught him looking her over with a longing expression. The look of surprise and discomfort on her face embarrassed him. He quickly lowered his head to Tim's letter in his lame hand, lost his place and read the last sentence.

...if not, I fear many of the youngsters I see in camp today will be in the hills tomorrow with guns. Write soon...Adios, Tim.

She called out to him. "I'm leaving, Ben!"
He turned to her by the open door. "Bonnie, wait! I want to talk to you."
She hesitated, then turned back and sat on the piano bench, running her hand slowly over the Baby Grand. He came and leaned on the piano, blushing.
He sighed. "I'm sorry I was gaping at you. I feel guilty, like I did something wrong. It makes me worry that my awkwardness around you might come between us... our friendship."
She kept her eyes and head lowered to the piano keys and her legs under the piano, away from his view.

He was still blushing. He straightened himself up. "We've known each other a long time." He wiped his brow. "I have these special feelings for you and for a long time I've had them. I won't let my thoughts get the better of me again; I'll control myself. Please don't feel uncomfortable or afraid to visit me at the bar. I'll miss you and our friendship if you do."

She looked at his red face. "Thanks for explaining yourself. I was worried."

Someone called out for a drink. She took her glass of ginger ale off the piano and drank all of what remained in the glass. She smiled at him and left the bar.

He went to his thirsty customer.

CHAPTER TWENTY FOUR

Brogan had been awake most of the night recording a message in both English and Spanish that would be broadcast over the Catholic radio stations in Central America. The message would anger many political groups in the region He knew that being an enemy of those groups was dangerous and, most often, fatal.

Dressed in khaki shorts, a white tee shirt, and wearing a Pittsburgh Pirate baseball cap, he walked in sandals through the refugee camp. Mesa Grande was stirring awake. Soon children would be running around the dusty tabletop surface of the campgrounds. The little ones would be safe as long as they stayed inside the barbed wire strands that marked the boundary of the United Nations Camp.

He walked between rows of tin-covered buildings that housed the refugees, kicking up dust in the strong wind. A heavy mist lingered on the mountains surrounding the Mesa. He expected the winds to soon bring heavy rain from the Caribbean.

Barefoot women were baking in one of the community ovens. As he drew close to them, they smiled and called out.

"¡Buenos días! ¿Cómo está usted, Padre?"

He waved to them. "Estoy bien, gracias." He rubbed his stomach. "¡Tengo hambre!"

The women laughed among themselves. One young woman held out a piece of bread and called out for him to come and take it from her hand. "¡Por favor! ¡Por favor!"

He went the short distance to her outstretched hand and took the warm bread.

"Muchas gracias," he said.

He ambled along the fence line. It was unguarded now, but at night the Honduran soldiers guarding the Mesa considered any shadowy movement outside the fence a guerilla, and would shoot to kill.

In the distance and below the Mesa, he could see the town of San Margos. He took Sarah's rosary from his shirt pocket and fingered the beads. But before he finished praying the beads, the first big drops of rain started falling causing puffs of dust to be hurled into the air. When he got back to his living quarters, he was dripping wet. Undressing and wiping himself dry, he put on a faded blue robe and placed the secret cassette into the recorder.

Soon after the sun went down, that cassette would be picked up by a lay leader of the church, a delegate who could be trusted to take the taped message back across the border into El Salvador and onto the Catholic Radio Station. He pushed the play button and sat on his cot.

Good evening. This is Father Tim Brogan speaking. I am a Roman Catholic Missionary at the Mesa Grande refugee camp. Last month I addressed an appeal to all foreign missionaries throughout Central America to enlist cooperation in spreading the word in favor of an American Government proposal that would allow the refugees of Mesa Grande to be repatriated to their beloved homeland. Under the American Plan, Japanese businesses would erect assembly plants in selected zones and employ the returning refugees. Modest wages and benefits would be earned by workers after an initial training period. I am now sad to report that I have reliable information of collusion between several Japanese Electronic Companies and some local government officials. Payoffs have taken place to restrict wages and benefits and perhaps more importantly, eliminate job security. Greed has been triumphant once again in this region of the world and I now urge anyone and everyone to withdraw their support of the American Plan...

Brogan poured himself a cup of cold black coffee from a battered metal coffee pot, and then sat the wobbly pot back down onto an electric hot plate. It started raining harder, pelting the tin roof, drowning out his taped voice. He sat on a square plastic container close to the wooden crate that he used as a table and bent his ear to the recording.

The refugees of Mesa Grande are rural people and have taken from the earth a living by farming on what land the rich and powerful have allotted them. Between farming and some occasional work given to them to clear land or cut sugar, they have been able to survive. Should they be repatriated to their villages now, at least they could continue to farm as they did in the past. Should they be trained to work in the proposed plants and resettled away from their villages, becoming dependent on assembly work for a livelihood, without job security, without fair compensation, they would only become enslaved to a system that's only purpose is to benefit others by...

The part of the tape that could cause his death was coming up. He put his ear closer to the spinning tape.

The proof I have of collusion in front of me is indisputable, and given to me by the most reliable sources inside of the El Salvadoran government who are friendly to the plight of their countrymen. I have copies of transactions from the Bank of Japan to the Bank of Panama depositing large sums of money into private bank accounts of government officials. I will now read the names of these officials and the numbers of their Panama Bank accounts...

He listened to the names, checking them off in his mind for correct pronunciation. He stopped the turning tape and stood up next to the plastic water jug. The jug was empty. He reminded himself to refill it later at the water trailer near the community ovens before nightfall. Even within the borders of the camp it was dangerous to go about needlessly in the dark. He exchanged tapes, slipping his Spanish speaking statement into the recorder. The rain let up. He sipped his cold coffee listening to himself repeat his message in Spanish.

After the cassette had concluded, he randomly picked up a cassette from the crate and replaced the Spanish statement with music. He reached and switched off the clear light bulb dangling from its insulated wire, which looped above around a ceiling support beam. Patsy Cline sang *Crazy* to him. He kicked off his sandals and lay on his cot. The taped messages were a death sentence. He had already been warned that his previous support for the American Plan had irritated the guerrillas. Now he would have all sides against him, the guerrillas and the governments.

When he was still endorsing the Plan, he knew he was placing a lot of faith in the United States to use its powerful influence in the region. And American funding was needed to provide the proper security for the assembly plants and workers to protect them against Leftist intimidation and violence. Now, by withdrawing his support for the Plan, he was telling the refugees that not even the most powerful nation in the world can control the flow of cash, and that they are better off with dirt floors and barbed wire than becoming industrial slaves to the rich of the world.

He was tired after being awake all night, but knew that sleep wouldn't come to him without aid. He reached beneath his hard pillow and took a pill from a small tin container. He had been using pills to find sleep since the American Plan began to unravel. The camp doctor gave him twenty-five tablets two weeks ago and he was already down to five. He swallowed the pill without water and listened to the cassette rewinding.

When he awoke, it was dusk. Patsy Cline was still singing. He stayed lying in his cot. Soon after sunset the Delegate would come for the tape. The nervous Delegate would not linger long after a single rap to his door. Death awaited the delegate, too, at any moment if a camp guard sighted his sneaky figure dodging about in the night.

With the darkening sky also came fears and doubts to his reasoning mind that soon he would be murdered. That he was giving up his blood for a fruitless cause. He thought about destroying the tapes and saying nothing in the future. Go back to Rivers Bend and Bonnie. Hide from the woes of this life and run to embrace its pleasures.

What would his speaking out matter in the long run of history? Nothing. Corruption was engraved in the fabric of the region, the world. The rich always exploited the poor. Why should he die for nothing? His blood would not change one life for the better, not erase one sin.

Destroy the tapes and live to go home to Bonnie. From Rivers Bend read about the campesinos etching out their daily bread and struggling to survive, to exist as individuals and families. Read about how they keep the faith, adore God. A God who could, with a sweeping thought, change the refugee's condition for the better, but just did not seem to give a damn. A God that doesn't care if Tim Brogan dies on a barren ridge in Honduras or in Bonnie's long smooth arms. He wished for Bonnie to be lying against him now, holding him in his loneliness, sharing in his indecision and agony.

He reached under his pillow and clutched Sarah's rosary and decided not to fight with God but not to pray to Him either. The signal rap came from the other side of the closed door.

In only minutes the delegate would flee from his risky task. A compulsion gripped Tim. He fumbled with Sarah's rosary, kissing it, rubbing it over his lips and sweating face. It was not an instrument of prayer, but a talisman, an amulet, calling upon Sarah's spirit, letting their love for each other rub his fear away and erase his urge to hide like a blind-to-the-world mole. He stood afraid and sweating.

Now he was leaving his Garden of Gethsemane. He stumbled to the door, started his walk to Calvary, his journey to death. Clutching the rosary as if holding Sarah's hand, he answered the rap at the door and handed the nervous shadow the cassettes that he sensed would become nails to crucify him.

CHAPTER TWENTY FIVE

The weather in Panama was predictable for August, hot and humid. The Marine guard snapped to attention, saluting Lynn as she approached the headquarters building of the United States Military Southern Command. Lynn, wearing her white dress uniform, returned the Marine's salute smartly and entered the building. She walked directly to the glass paneled door identifying the Office of Naval Intelligence. Inside she was greeted by her Commanding Officer sitting behind a Navy gray metal desk. The Captain remained sitting while smiling at Lynn.

"Lieutenant, prompt as usual."

"Thank you, sir."

"Sit down, Lynn," the Captain was motioning to a sturdy oak chair to one side of his desk. "Coffee?"

She sat in the hard chair at attention, feet together, back straight, looking at the Caption.

"No, thank you, sir."

"Lynn," the Captain said, correcting his posture, sitting up straight and picking up a large manila envelope from his desk and handing it to her. "Can you identify anyone in these enlarged photos?"

She opened the envelope and removed the pictures. She sat the glossy colored photos on her lap shuffling through them slowly. She lifted her eyes and looked at the Captain. "Yes, I can, sir."

"Who can you positively identify?"

"He's younger, but its Father Brogan, I'm certain. A Catholic missionary."

The Captain smiled.

Lynn glanced back down at the photos. "Who's the Oriental woman? Japanese?"

The Captain nodded. "Yes, but that's not important, Lieutenant. Do you know where Father Brogan is now?'

"I'm not sure."

The Captain told her. "At the Mesa Grande refugee camp."

"I didn't know. The last time I saw him, he was teaching Spanish at a seminary in New York."

The Captain leaned back in his swivel chair, placed his hands behind his neck and stared past Lynn to the American flag on a staff in the corner of the room.

"When you were assigned to Naval Intelligence, Lynn, the Navy did a background check on you and your family. This Father Brogan is listed in that investigation as a friend of your family. You even put his name down as a reference, Lieutenant."

"I did, sir."

The Captain rocked back and forth in his swivel chair. "We fed Father Brogan's name into our computer, and bingo, to our surprise, he turns out to be a friend of one of our own. Anyhow..." The Captain quit rocking, leaned forward, laid his arms on his desk and crossed them. "That's not important. What is important is this priest, this Father Timothy Brogan, has taken it upon himself to undermine the American Plan for the economic development and repatriation program for the Mesa Grande refugees."

"I wasn't aware of Tim's activities, sir. My assignments since coming to the Canal have, for the most part, been drug investigations."

The Captain chuckled. "I know, Lynn, we're kicking you upstairs to more important matters." The Captain chuckled again. "Politics."

The Captain pushed away from his desk and leaned back into his comfortable chair.

"Lieutenant, this priest must stop opposing the Plan. It is of vital importance to the government of El Salvador that the refugees return home. Living in refugee camps only reinforces their discontent, and the refugees are a continuous recruiting haven for the guerrillas. You know about the American Plan for work zones that would provide jobs for the repatriated refugees?"

Lynn shifted inside her hard oak chair. "Yes, sir, a routine brief only."

The Captain ran his hand over the top of his gray crew cut. "Well, Father Brogan thought the Plan was a grand idea a while ago. He even sent his thoughts about it over the air on the Catholic Radio Station not long ago. Now he has changed his mind. This priest is very influential with the campesinos and has a long record of service to the cause of the underprivileged."

Lynn shifted in her chair. "What changed his mind, sir?"

The Captain frowned. "Listen to his message, his recent broadcast on the Catholic Radio."

The Captain turned on a cassette recorder to the side of his desk. While the tape played, the Captain poured himself a cup of coffee from a pot on the stand behind her. He stayed out of her sight while the tape played.

She listened intently to Tim's voice. The recording ended and the Captain returned to his desk and turned off the cassette player. He remained standing, holding his steaming cup of coffee in front of himself and smiling down at her. "Well, what do you think, Lieutenant?"

Lynn did not hesitate in giving him her answer. "I think he is right. Are there payoffs?"

"Lynn, this is Central America. Kickbacks are a way of life."

She wiggled in her chair. Her backside ached. "Then Father Brogan is right. In the long run, the refugees will be worse off."

"Lynn, in every American city there are kickbacks."

She was becoming suspicious. Her Commanding Officer was aware of her discomfort, yet, was purposely choosing to see her in an uncomfortable hurting position. Her backside was turning numb.

"I know that, sir. But it is not a way of life condoned from top to bottom in government."

The Captain sipped his coffee and walked behind Lynn, speaking as she looked straight ahead. "You're correct. Corruption is a continuous thing, which is why our government wishes the Plan to proceed. After the refugees are back home, working at the plants, then our government can put pressure on to improve the working conditions of the campesinos."

She spoke up. "What if our government doesn't..."

She was cut off by the Captain in a voice more authoritarian. "Lieutenant, this isn't supposed to be a discussion of who is and who isn't right or wrong!"

The Captain walked back to his desk without his coffee cup, sat in his chair and shuffled some papers.

The hard oak chair did indeed have a purpose, she thought to herself. Agree with all of the Captain's propaganda; get out of the chair fast. Slow learners get a callused ass.

"Your assignment, Lieutenant, is to arrange a meeting with this priest, persuade him to back off. We are not requesting that he approve the Plan, just keep his damn mouth shut and do what a priest is supposed to do. Say Mass, hear confessions, whatever!"

"What am I supposed to do with these pictures?" Blackmail him?"

The Captain grinned. "Not exactly. Father Brogan must stop meddling. Those photos you are holding, if distributed, will embarrass the church and Father Brogan. If he loves his church, ask him to spare it unnecessary embarrassment. It seems that your Father Tim had a few good times in the Navy. If the photos do not quiet him...he'll be killed."

She gasped. "By us?"

"By any number of people including the Leftists who remember his first radio message in support of the American Plan. The Leftists don't want fair wages any more than the rich and powerful. Happy campesinos don't want to fight. So, you see, Lynn, we can only do so much. Sweet talk this man into using his common sense. We don't want anymore Cuban state of affairs in this hemisphere. That's not good for the United States."

She lost all feeling in her lower back and buttocks, but was determined to have her say. "For the record sir, I think Father Brogan is right. When the campesinos get back..."

The Captain cut her off. "That's out of our power, Lieutenant! Take the photographs, meet with this friend of your family and report the results of that meeting back to this office. That is all. Dismissed."

She slowly rose, straightened her sore back, and brought her feet together to the position of attention. "Aye, aye, sir." With short painful steps, she left the office.

Her quarters had the basic government furniture issued a junior officer; a single bed, dresser, closet, two chairs, nightstand, and lamp. Now, in the privacy of her lodgings and standing under the overhead light, she studied the photos more closely.

Of the six pictures, four showed Tim in a compromising situation. Two were of him and the Japanese woman sitting close together and looking into each others eyes. A bottle of whiskey and partially filled glasses were on a table in front of them.

The four photos that could harm him the most were in a different setting. In three of them, he was partially naked on a bed, with the girl provocatively dressed standing over him. The last picture had them both naked and lying across the bed.

She put the pictures back inside the envelope and tossed them on the floor. She undressed to her slip and stretched out on her back across the bed. Her lower back was still aching from the Captain's chair.

She would have to catch a military flight to the Honduran capital city, Tegucigalpa. From there, the Honduran National Guard could transport her to the refugee camp. She rolled onto her stomach and reached for the telephone on the nightstand.

CHAPTER TWENTY SIX

The dust stirred up by the Jeep ride to the Mesa was still hanging heavy in the hot air. Brown clouds obscured the campesinos gathering around the visitors. Lynn's white sneakers got soiled as soon as she stepped onto the Mesa. And once the floating dirt settled back down onto the ground, she kicked a Jeep tire to clear them of dust. The afternoon sunshine was hot and brightly reflected off her yellow slacks and matching sleeveless blouse.

She was ordered to wear civilian clothes on her assignment inside the United Nations camp and to be careful not to connect the United States Military with that body of world nations. Her two escorts were alert and uncomfortable being taken into the midst of so many unhappy campesinos. The refugees' dark eyes stared in silence at the two National Guardsman dressed in their pressed uniforms and U.S. made weapons at the ready.

She recognized Tim making his way through the growing throng of refugees, a baseball cap on top of his smiling head. When she could see him entirely in his Bermuda shorts and faded tee shirt, she went at him smiling. They hugged and held each other for a long moment. Then he studied her at arm's length and shouted to the assembly, "Amante!"

She looked up, smiling into his tan handsome face. "Stop it! You're in enough trouble without shouting that I'm your sweetheart."

"Not with you, I hope?"

"No, I'm here to save your life. Can we go somewhere, talk in private?"

"About my broadcast?"

She shook her head and spoke softly. "Yes, Tim."

"Come on, we'll go to my quarters."

She went to the Jeep and got her briefcase. He took her by the arm and guided her to his tin-covered shed. Once inside, he opened his only folding chair and put it next to the wooden crate, motioning for her to sit down. He took the tape recorder off of the crate and sat it on his cot. He sat on the plastic container.

Looking solemn; she opened her briefcase and began her mission by handing him the photographs.

He shuffled through them one by one several times before speaking in a whisper. "Blackmail?"

She never took her eyes from him and answered in an even voice. "Yes, Tim. But, for what it's worth, I personally agree with your present position."

He stared at the photographs.

"Tim, they're not asking you to retract anything that you've said, only to remain silent on the subject from now on."

His voice hardened. "They?"

"The governments. Ours, the El Salvadorians, the Hondurans. And Tim, the guerillas aren't happy with you either."

He shook his head slightly but said nothing.

She reached across the table and touched his hand. "They'll kill you if you don't listen to me and continue to broadcast."

He dropped the pictures onto the crate, took her hand into his own, and looked at her tenderly. "I used to date your mother. I lived with her for awhile."

Lynn was taken aback by what the priest said, but he continued to stare at her and speak of Sarah.

"This was before John came into your mother's life. You were very small." He gave her a weak smile. "Becoming a missionary was my second choice. Sarah, in a roundabout way, sent me here to this Mesa. I never stopped loving your mother. I still think of her every day."

His eyes glistened. Lynn squeezed his hand.

"Sarah always believed me to be different than the other men we grew up with around Rivers Bend, but I wasn't. On my visits to your family over the many years since Sarah and I parted, I sensed from your mother that I was her burning bush, her wishing well. That maybe through me something good would come out of our lost romance." He paused and reached for the towel draped over the foot of his bed. He removed his ball cap and wiped the sweat from his face.

She watched him scrub his face but said nothing. She understood that he was doing therapy on himself, unloading pestering thoughts that were inside him for a long time. She wanted to talk about what she had been sent to Mesa Grande for, but in his present state of mind, he would be deaf to any requests she might ask of him. He threw the towel on his cot and started talking again in a flat even tone.

"I live with more inner conflict with each passing day. I get doubts about God, my church, even Christianity itself. Most often the battle in my mind resolves nothing that hasn't already been thought out by people more brilliant than I." he swallowed. His mouth was dry.

"All my life I've had a desire to put things straight with the world. It all seemed so simple to me. Jesus taught the way, the light, and the truth. People didn't even have to think, just follow the instructions handed down by Christ's Apostles and martyrs. All I have determined after years of studying and thinking is that I don't know for certain that God exists. The same answer I would have tucked away in my brain if I'd never opened a book or made the sign of the cross."

He stood, "Want water, Lynn? Sorry, no ice."

She nodded. "Please."

He filled two big glasses to the brim and handed one to her. She drank half of it before setting it on the crate. He drank all of his water before sitting back down.

"To discontinue my protest now against this planned manipulation of the poor would be to betray Sarah's trust in my calling, her faith in my courage. I think of her and some others in my past whenever I need to gather up courage and be brave. By loving Sarah, if only in memory, I become bolder and more gallant than I really am. For over twenty years, I've held symbols and wore vestments proclaiming I was a follower of Christ. To abandon Jesus' teaching now would place me in Nicodemus' shadow, acknowledging Jesus only in the safety and cover of darkness. I cannot..." Tim stopped suddenly, apologized.

"I'm sorry, Lynn. I went too far with my thoughts."

Lynn again pleaded with him. "Please, Tim, don't speak out again, that is all they are asking."

"Why not ask for my soul?" Tim grunted and then spoke of his own wishes.

"Should I be killed, Lynn, I want to be buried in the priest plot at Saint James Cemetery. Please inform my superiors if I should be murdered before I have an opportunity to write them myself. Traditionally, we missionaries are buried where we drop. I would like to be buried back home, near Sarah and others I loved." Again a weak smile quickly passed over his lips. "A romantic to the end."

"Stop this coffin talk." she scolded him. "Nothing is going to happen if you do as I ask."

He didn't answer her and seemed in a daze. The only sounds came from the outside. She was not sweating as much as him. His face was taut and soaked with sweat and fear.

She spoke, still scolding him. "At least think about it, before rushing off another cassette to the Catholic radio station!"

It was over for him. The dark mood falling from his mind like a theater curtain coming down at the end of a morbid play. He stood and smiled down at her. "Now, that is something I can promise you. No more tapes. I had my say. There's no more I can do. Whatever happens...happens."

"Then I leave here with assurances...there will be no more interferences by you?"

"If I agree to that statement, your superiors will think I capitulated to the photos, the blackmail. I wouldn't want them to think that. I won't interfere anymore because there is truthfully nothing more I can do. And anyhow, I'm leaving here soon...going back to the states. My mission here is completed. You report that to the top brass."

He changed the subject. "How long can you stay?"

"I have to leave soon to make my flight connections."

"Do you have time for a quick tour of the camp?"

She sighed. "Not really." She looked into his pleading eyes. "I'll make time."

He became exuberant. "Great!"

He led her about the grounds, introducing her like a proud Daddy to the shabbily dressed brown smiling refugees. The children jumped at them playfully and were overjoyed with a pat on the head from the handsome couple.

During her tour of duty in the Canal Zone, her contact with the local citizens was always official or in client-customer transactions. The display of warmth and love the campesinos gave Tim and her by association with him, delighted her and aroused within her the caring femininity that she forgot she possessed.

The refugees became human to her as she laughed with them, touched them, listened to the stories of desperate flight from their villages, and loss of loved ones in the violent social struggle inside of their country. Their plight was real to her now and not only words on intelligence briefs back at headquarters. She reached up and took his hand from her arm and held it tight.

Now she had her answer. Her mission was a failure. He lied to her. He would keep fighting the Plan and would broadcast again if he thought it would help the refugees. They walked hand in hand to the barbed wire fence, gazing down the slopes towards San Margo's.

Lynn asked without facing him. "Who's the girl?"

"A bar girl. I met her on a port call in Japan. Actually through John."

She became wide-eyes and gaped at him. "My Dad took those photos?"

He frowned. "No! One of his Japanese friends clicked them. I'm pretty sure. Pretty drunk I was. We all were. The question I have is how did Naval Intelligence get them?"

She clenched her teeth. "Damn! It was Orson! It had to be! He took Dad's Marine Corps memorabilia to storage for me." she grimaced. "The government recently did a background investigation on you. Must have had an investigator go to Rivers Bend and sought out people that knew you. It had to be Orson."

He shook his head staring down the ridge. "What an Orson world I live in. I see nothing but hate anymore."

She let go of his hand, reached out, and turned his face to her. "Unlike you, Tim, I know there are still a lot of good people in the world. I think perhaps you have been in too many wretched camps like Mesa Grande in your lifetime and you tend to lose sight of the good being done right before your eyes. Work like you and the other missionaries are doing here in Central America. You're too close to your own fire to see how far the light is glowing." She took his hand again. "And that, Father Brogan, concludes my sermon. I must go. Please be careful. Pray more and broadcast less for the sake of all of us that love you."

He chuckled. "I hate to kneel. Always did."

She winked at him. "Perhaps God doesn't want men like you on their knees?"

"Meaning?"

"That God has heroes too, and maybe you're one of them."

"I love you too." Tim laughed.

She lifted his hand to her lips and kissed it. "I've got to go."

Without another word, they walked in the bright sunshine across the dusty mesa to the waiting guardsman and the hot Jeep. They kissed goodbye.

CHAPTER TWENTY SEVEN

During the week following Lynn's visit to Mesa Grande, Tim sent off a letter to her. He wrote his letter to her in a deprecating way, joking about his graveside mood, and how he put his reservations for burial in the priest plot at Saint James cemetery through a Naval Intelligence officer. He promised Lynn not to be as somber when they met again. He also revealed to her his plans about leaving the priesthood and marrying Bonnie.

He stopped at the camp fence line. Crackling birds were pleasing him with their short sounds in the morning air. It was cool on the Mesa, and the breeze felt good on his tan bare back. He took Bonnie's letter from the back pocket of his Bermuda shorts. He had already read the long letter many times and now in a melancholy mood read parts of it again, skipping over the paragraph about Gypsy's burning death. He wanted to stay cheerful.

...I love you, my very own Don Quixote. I cannot blow the numbers off of my calendar fast enough to get to September when you will be back at the seminary and shortly afterwards with me forever. I lie in bed every night remembering our last time together and the thrill of waking up in your arms...When are you telling your superiors that you're resigning from their club? I know it will be an emotional hell for you to utter those words, 'I quit' and I wish I could be there for you when you do. Until my last breath, Tim, I'll be with you, for you and desire you! As soon as you give me the word, I'm going to plan our little wedding. Everything but who will perform the ceremony. I also understand that will be a heartbreaker for you. I have thought about it. I have an idea; that after a simple civil ceremony, we will have Father Eugene give us his blessing.

...I'm going to wear white (of course), a short but respectable dress, a white hat and no veil. I want to make sure you see who you are marrying! You are my sun, Tim. My days are full of you, and at night I dream of you. I feel blessed beyond my capability and thank God for bringing me this happiness. Let the walkman I sent sing my praises to you!"

He folded the letter and returned it to his back pocket and then took the walkman from the back of his neck and fitted the earphones over his ears. Life stirred inside of his body thinking of Bonnie. If only Rome modernized its view of the clergy, allowing priests to marry, he could have Bonnie here on the Mesa working beside him as his wife. Some grief came upon him with those wishful thoughts and he turned to music from the walkman to lighten his heart. Nat King Cole sang to him.

He wiped his brow with his palm. It was warming up. He took Sarah's rosary from his side pants pocket, decided against praying at the moment, and only held the beads in his hand. He walked slowly, gazing at the dusty ground ahead of him, listening to the sweet music. He didn't hear or see the birds behind him when they quit crying out moments before they flew in a flock from their hiding places in the bush.

A strange feeling came over him. He thought somebody was watching him. He turned and looked through the wire fence. A young man dressed in black stood up among the bushes. Tim instantly knew the man was on a mission and vice-gripped Sarah's rosary. He arrived at his Calvary.

The smashing impact of the bullets into his bare stomach and chest knocked him off his feet. He crashed on his back in the thick dust. Dusty air consumed his body in brown fog. Bonnie's gift was still playing, Nat singing softly into his ears.

Suddenly a face was looking into his. He recognized him as a camp helper. The campesino was screaming to the others gathering around his broken body. The gawking campesinos looked frightened. Women were screaming, crying, wailing to God for mercy.

He wanted to get up, onto his feet, but his legs would not move.

The camp helper kept shouting to the enlarging crowd, waving his hands at them to stay back, away from the bloody missionary.

Tim started groping his chest and stomach. Moving bits of flesh about as he slid his fingers along in the blood. A small boy standing in the crowd saw the red beads lying in the dust. Picking up the dusty rosary with his small brown fingers, the boy put the beads into Tim's searching hand.

Tim smiled at the lad. The boy smiled back.

EPILOGUE

Tim's grave lay in the late afternoon shadow of the Jesus statue hovering over the priest plot. Layers of colorful fall leaves from the tree-lined cemetery road covered the ground.

The two friends stood over the mound of settling dirt. At Bonnie's request, Ben always accompanied her to visit Tim's grave. Since Tim's funeral, two weeks is the longest they stayed away from the cemetery.

They stood in silence, not praying, not crying, only staring at the mound of earth. They always stood for the longest time before Bonnie would give a heavy sigh, and only then would they leave. She dressed up for each visit to Tim's grave. Today, in the early October chill, she wore a dark dress suit. Her dyed brown hair braided. Ben wore the same suit each time. His only remaining suitable attire.

Bonnie sighed. "I'm ready."

Ben took her by the arm and they turned towards the road and Bonnie's car. They walked close together, taking small steps down the hilly leaf-covered slope.

Ben stopped, and held her in place by the arm. "Bonnie, I'm leaving Rivers Bend. Selling the Piano Bar to Dutch."

She looked up into his brooding face. "Where will you go?"

"I'm not sure."

She looked back down at the rotting leaves. "Have you finalized the sale?"

"No, I'm meeting with Dutch tonight."

"Ben, why not remodel? Brighten the place up. Hire a piano player. If there is anything that I have learned in my life, Ben, it's that people will always find a dollar for beer and moody music. People need to feel like they're alive, and who can do that better than a piano man?"

"But Bonnie, I know that. I don't have the money to do what you ask. I know things will get better. There is even talk of tearing the steel mill down and building an industrial park on the site. I don't have the cash to see me through to better times. I'm broke."

"I'm not!" Bonnie snapped and started walking again down the slope. "I'll lend you the money."

Ben followed after her talking. "Ahh...I don't know, Bonnie. I'm a loser. I'd hate to lose your money."

"What about a partnership?" she asked. "I'll put up the money. You put up the Piano Bar." They reached the road.

"Thanks, Bonnie, but if it didn't work out, I'd feel terrible."

She slapped his small arm. "Quit worrying! Two losers like us. Hell, our luck is bound to change."

Ben opened the passenger door for her. He always drove her to the cemetery. He got in behind the steering wheel and started the motor and looked over at her. "It's getting better for you, I can tell."

She slid a little closer to him. "Yeah it is, and I'm tired of mourning." she snickered. "Serves him right leaving my bed and running off into the jungle." She put her hand on Ben's thigh. He blushed and put the car in gear and drove off.

Bonnie smiled and got personal. "Have you ever slept with a woman?"

He turned ruby red.

She giggled. "I didn't think so. Do you still like me?"

He nodded without looking at her.

She laughed hard and looked him over. "Get yourself down to one hundred and eighty pounds, untarnished one, and I'll marry you."

He almost drove off the road, stopping the car before it went into a small ditch. "Do you mean it?"

"I do…I do!" she screamed. "I feel like doing something completely crazy…just to know I'm alive…And to think I'll have a virgin on my honeymoon and a piano bar to come back home too. Who could ask for more?"

He was stunned into numbness by the sudden turn of events in his life. All he ever dreamed of was coming true and in a rush of emotion he bent and kissed her quickly on the lips.

She quipped. "You'll need some training. And lose the mustache!"

The End

ABOUT THE AUTHOR

Enlisting as a private in the United States Marine Corps only days after his seventeenth birthday, Ambrose remained a Marine for twenty years, serving in the United States, the Caribbean, Asia, and on the high seas. He retired a Marine Captain and lives in Western Pennsylvania with his wife, Doris.